Unlovable Bitch

A Novel By

Allysha Hamber

UNLOVABLE BITCH®

UNLOVABLE BITCH

Published by: CreateSpace.com
Written by: Allysha Hamber
Edited by: Dolly Lopez
Cover design by: Allysha L. Hamber

For information contact:
Allysha Hamber
Email: Lele4you@hotmail.com
Website: www.myspace.com/allyshahamber

ISBN: 9781440421297

Dedication

This book, as with every positive thing I do in life, is for my babies... my Princes, Dorian Jones and Davion Hamber, along with my princess, Tamara Hamber. My heart will always, always belong to you! Momma loves you very, very much! Nothing or no one has the power to ever change that!

R.I.P. to my big cousin, Alvin Johnson, Jr. who lost his life, January 17, 2009. No More Pain, No More Sorrow... finally, you are at peace. Please know, you are *forever* gone but you *never* forgotten! Love Ya!

-Ya Baby Cuz, Lysha

Doin' It A Little Different

We gon' do a lil something different this time around. Usually this is where I shout out all the people I think deserves it but this time, it's time for a change. I feel as though I am beginning a new journey in my life. One that is filled with lessons and experiences that I can't help but thank God that He and He alone, brought me through. I'm a realist and in being so, I am woman enough to admit when I've made mistakes in life and used bad judgment.

With that said, I have to admit that since I've been home from prison, I have been one of the most Naïve women that have walked the face of the earth. I have always believed that "if you treat people the way you want to be treated," they have no choice but to treat you the same way in return. I have learned the hard way that something my Grandmother told me along time ago, still reigns true, now more than ever.

"Everybody has an ulterior motive for wanting to be apart of your life. It can be a good one or a bad one, but everybody's got one."

I have come to know the face-to-face meaning of "a wolf in sheep's clothing." I surrounded myself with people I thought wanted the best for me, at least they pretended too. Until I made decisions that didn't fit with what "they" thought I should do and then, look out!

The HATIN' began and it's grown stronger and stronger. Which now, I'm thankful for, because it has motivated me to better. To reach even higher to achieve my goals. To dream more, to laugh more and most of all, it has taught me that "if I let them change the person I am, they win." And I'm not a loser.

I came home from prison, so full of hope and promise. I had my mind set on what I wanted to do and accomplish. But because I still had an underlying need to be loved by people in general, that need led me right into the pathway of people I knew didn't deserve to be apart of my world. I was still searching for someone to care about me and the things I had been through. Just for the sake of feeling like, I "belonged." But guess what? It no longer has the power to hurt me. The situation nor the people involved in the situations. Simply because I did exactly what God wanted me to do, I learned from it, I've grown from it and for that, I am thankful.

So, with that said, to those who are no longer here for whatever reason it may be, I thank you anyway because somewhere along the road in my life, you meant something to me, so it's all good. This time, I am gonna shout all the HATERS because without ya'll, I would've never made the choice to be better than you, I would've settled and been content with being just like you.

So... Shouts out to...

My family: Don't get it twisted, this don't just include some of them DNA's of mine but some folks I thought was like fam' but really are just ready-made hata's. It hurts me that most of the negative things I hear on the streets comes back to me via you all's mouth. It is crazy to hear, "Yo' people dog you out to the fullest." We got the same blood line in some instances, but I must be of a different breed cause I don't feel the need to make myself look better, by makin' ya'll look bad and doggin' ya'll out. I don't need to put ya'll's business in the street. I'm better than that. It seems like every positive step I make, ya'll wanna see me fall back four but guess what, It won't happen. I have learned to live with the negative, so please, keep hatin' on me, I don't care, in fact, I invite it... it only makes me stronger.

To the "Block,"... Ya'll too damn grown to do the wack ass shit ya'll do to each other. Real bad boys... Real G's, move in silence. Guess some of ya'll never leaned that part of the game. I've leaned a lot from ya'll but the greatest lesson is: "MISSERY LOVES COMPANY!!!!"

Now… My Thank You's…

Those who stood by me (The one's who been real.)

My Blood: Punkin (Big Gurl), Rhonda (Boobie) LaNelle (Lynn) and my one and only, Big Pimpin'… My baby brother Sleezy (Slug). My nieces and nephews, Vincell, I love you all, always remember that. I ain't about to drop all these names and show love and then these be the same ones that don't even come to the book release party! What part of the game is that? Anywayz: A new year and a new crew… Anthony(Tony D)Johnson, 104.1 FM Family, DJ Pat Precise, DJ Bishop V Luv, Officer Trey Green (what's up Boo-Boo?), Ms. Mariah Richardson, Ms. Linda (hang in there girl!) My number one fans, Ms. Red & Ms. Lynn (Keep holdin' it down for me! I'm taking ya'll to Oprah with me!)

To my friends: Jay… what can I say? Love u always! Ronald Macon (Much love, you have always been supportive and unbiased in all the shit that goes on around here, I love you for that.) Kokomo A.K.A L.A.W, keep doin' what you do… Always got place in my heart!), Jayson Lambert, Shannon Rucker, Jean Whitby (Hey Sissy… Thanks for all your love and support. Over the years you have always been good to me and I will always love you and your family for life.) Momma Whitby (You've been in my heart from day one. Opened up your family to me and words can't express how much I love you!), Mary Wilson (Thank you for all your love and support, may God continue to shine down upon you and all you do!).

Last but certainly not least… My Heavenly father, who has brought me through another storm. I know why I must go through these tests. To make me stronger and better. The tears have dried, the storms have passed and the sun is on the horizon. Thank You for bringing me through it all, still in my right mind. Undamaged by the winds of hatred, jealousy, envy, greed and misery. I'm Thankful for the fact that no matter how many men, I foolishly have opened my legs too, You have brought me through it all, free and clean of any disease. That through molestation, You let me survive with a sane mind. That by being sent to prison, You turned it for my good by showing me all the gifts you planted inside me. That in the mist of losing my children, You and You alone, are returning them to me one-by-one.

To those who have hurt me in the past, I forgive you. To those I have hurt in the past, whether it's been an unkind word, sleeping with yo' man or yo' husband, gossiping about you or anything that I shouldn't have done, I ask you for forgiveness as well. My future looks bright and I pray yours look the same!

Unlovable Bitch

What about me is so unlovable, that people simply
won't understand?
I've wracked my brain from front to back and thought
of everything that I can.
I've worn out my body for money, I've tried to gain
love by working my lips.
See a prospect in the vicinity and immediately add an
extra wiggle to my hips.
I've been beat down and abused, in everyway misused
but still, I keep on trying.
Always on my back, turning tricks for money stacks
but inside my soul is dying.
Been hit with a fist more times than I can count, my eyes
and my jaws stay swollen.
On the streets you mean nothin', you gain no one's respect,
when out there on the hoe strollin'.
But if you'll take a minute to peel back the layers of the
woman you see, beaten down by life,
You'll bare witness to the itch.
An itch, that only real love, in time can scratch
away but until then, I'm forever…
an ***Unlovable Bitch****.*

Prelude...

What about me is so bad that people continuously wanna hurt me? Why won't anybody love me?

Dream pondered this thought as she squeezed her eyes together tightly and winched at the intensity of the pain between her thighs. It was hot—so hot, that Dream could have sworn that the tears falling from her eyes were made of pure steam.

Pieces, her pimp, was angry that Dream had lost his money for the second time that week to yet, another trick.

The day had started off promising for Dream. Her goal was to turn enough tricks in order to pay both Pieces his cut and still have enough money to rent a better room for her and her infant daughter. Maybe, finally move into an affordable apartment of her own. Nevertheless, by the stroke of six o'clock, the day had quickly steamrolled downhill. Her last customer of the day did his best to make sure of that.

Silently, the tears rolled down her face as Frank, one of her once a month customers, beat down upon her used-up vagina with his disgusting flesh. His heavy, two-hundred sixty-five pound body slammed down consistently against her frail, young frame. His breathing was labored, an indication that he had finally reached his quest. Dream's tears were symbolic of the emptiness, the pain and the shame she felt inside.

He was her eleventh trick of the day. Her vaginal lips were swollen and irritated from a long day's work. The muscles in her jaws were tired from the service six of them had demanded. Yet, Dream somehow managed to take comfort in knowing her baby girl had a roof over her head and her stomach was full from the pay.

Dream's body hurt like hell, her heart hurt... her soul hurt. What was the alternative? They had nowhere else to go. No family to take them in. For Dream, this was it, this was life... this was survival.

As the overweight customer, undoubtedly high on heroin, injected her with his disgrace, he rolled over, panting slowly and barked, "Go get me a glass of water!"

He exhaled strongly as Dream crawled from under the covers and headed for the bathroom. It felt as if someone had literally kicked her between her legs.

"That shol' is some good pussy you got there gal. If you ain't good for nothing else, you know you damn good fo' that."

Dream thought back to the first time she'd heard that from a man and frowned.

Fuck You! Dream spat out as she filled the dirty glass with water. She watched sadly as her tears began to mix with the swirling crystal liquid going down the rusty drain. She wished like hell that she too, could slide down into the tiny hole and disappear. As the two clear liquids blended, you could no longer tell where Dream's tears ended and the water began. As it was with every aspect of her life.

Where did the pain end? Where did peace and happiness begin?

"Let the water run some mo'. I want my shit real cold," he commanded.

While the water flowed from the faucet, Dream grabbed the soiled, dingy white washcloth from the towel rack and wet it underneath the coolness of the faucet water. She gingerly sat down on the crooked and cracked toilet seat, spread her legs apart and placed the rag onto her vagina lips as the tears continued to flow from her eyes.

As Dream rested on the broken fixture, she continued

to wet the cloth and apply it to the creases between her thighs to hold down the swelling.

In the distance, she heard the door to the hotel room close. She quickly reached over, turned off the squeaky faucet and exited the bathroom. She looked around the dimly lit room but there was no sign of her customer; he was gone. Her eyes quickly darted over to the dresser, searching for her sixty-dollar payment; thirty for the head she given him and another thirty for the pussy she set out. It wasn't there.

She checked underneath the lamp and the pillows on the bed. All turned up empty. She looked over to the brown and orange sofa to see her blue secondhand purse, lying open.

Her heart sank and her stomach turned into knots as she picked up her coin purse from beside the rubble. Not only was her trick gone and had slipped out without paying her, but he had also stolen all of the money from her purse as well.

She angrily threw the coin purse down onto the floor and plopped down onto the soiled linen at the corner of the bed.

"Fuck! That's the second time this week! Pieces is gon' kill me! What the fuck am I gon' do now?"

Dream slowly rose from the bed and walked over to the dresser. She flicked a cockroach off her clothes, slid on her dingy beige bra and crusted beige panties. Despite the pain between her legs, Dream knew she'd have to go back out on the streets to make up Pieces' money, if not a dime more. He had let her slide once before when she'd come up short, with a promise she'd make it back up for him later in the week.

She put on her blue and white striped mini-skirt with its matching halter-top. It was her attention getter. She brushed her hair back into a banana clip and tried to fix up her face. Her eyes were swollen and dark red from crying. At seventeen, Dream's skin already showed signs of aging. She looked used up... she was used up and she was tired.

The room rent was due by twelve the next afternoon, which meant that Dream had a little less than twelve hours to recover Pieces' money and make enough for food, rent and diapers.

She walked over and knelt down beside the worn dresser drawer, she had tried to make into a comfortable bed for her three-month-old daughter, Destiny. She was still sleeping soundly as she reached inside her diaper to make sure she was dry. Dream lifted the drawer onto the bed so the roaches were less likely to crawl on her, grabbed her purse, shut the door behind her and went back out into the night. As usual, she said a silent wish, a wish that someone would kill her and take the pain away.

The night had ended with Dream only making one hundred and eighty dollars. Three tricks were all she could handle because of the swelling of her vagina lips and walls. She knew she had to face Pieces and tell him what happened again, and she knew this time he probably wouldn't believe her.

So many times the girls on the streets used the story of being robbed by a customer as an excuse for not having his money. Usually it was because they were feeding a habit such as crack cocaine or boy and Dream knew Pieces would be fed up. She was right.

Pieces now towered above her, with her legs spread apart and her ankles bound to each corner of her old broken down, squeaky bed. Her hands were laced together by a dingy, twisted brown and white rope.

In Pieces eyes, he had been lenient with Dream once before and now he felt that she needed to be made an example of to the other young girls that he had out on the streets working for him.

In the pimping game, hoes took kindness for weakness and Pieces firmly believed that if you let them get over once, they would think it was okay to come at you with every bullshit excuse they could think of, as to why they didn't have your money. Therefore, Pieces allowed no margin for error. The only reason he'd let Dream slip by without beating her the first time was that she had made him a lot of money and he knew she had the unconditional grind inside of her back then.

However, once she experienced motherhood, in Pieces eye, her priorities became confused and getting him his money was no longer her main objective. So this time, he had to make a statement to her, just as he had done to Ebony.

Pieces had heated the tip of his nine-millimeter Beretta for the third time over the flame of the burning candle and inserted it into the bruised up vagina of Dream's battered body. Her left eye was swollen shut from his fist, and her right jaw experienced the same as her blood gushed from her mouth after she had served him on demand with her lips.

Dream looked over at the desolate creature crawling up the cracked, heavily stained wall of her rented room in the Jefferson Arms in downtown St. Louis. She envied the small creature at that very moment. Envied its ability to move when it wanted, go where it wanted and shield itself from danger as it wanted. She envied its freedom. It was something she had never known in her life before. True freedom was a luxury that she had never felt.

Growing up in the Darst Webb Projects of St. Louis, Dream was born to a mother who lived for the street life. At the age of thirty-three and the mother of three young girls,

Dream's mother Karen, was a street whore in a different sense of the word.

Working as a Pharmacy Technician by day and a stripper by night, Karen rarely saw the inside of their home she shared with her three children. Dream and her sister's were often left to fend for themselves, knocking on their neighbors' doors in the project to ask for food, bathroom tissue and other necessities.

Dream was the youngest of the siblings and often found herself alone most of the time in the rough neighborhood. Her older sisters were often busy, running with their cliques, which left Dream vulnerable to the salt of the streets.

Dream's life changed dramatically after her father, Jerome died in a shootout in the Peabody Projects at the age of 34. He was the only person Dream felt safe around, and when Jerome died, Dream often felt she lost her life as well.

For Dream, Jerome's death was the beginning of a life full of both hell and misery. And as she screamed out in agony, the hot steel continuously blistering her now seventeen-year-old bloodied vagina, she reflected on the morning her life had changed from a life of promise, to a nightmare of despair...

Chapter One

Her virgin blood was everywhere. On the sheets, her pastel pink pajama gown and flowing freely from between her legs. Dream could barely move from the pain. The pain throbbed and pulsated throughout her body like she'd been beaten with a hammer. In some ways, she wished she'd had. Anything was better than the mental confusion and the emotional anguish she felt at that very moment.

His message was verbally clear, yet inside her nine-year-old mind, it had somehow been both entangled and crossed.

"Get up and go take a bath. Change that bed and clean up this room. And if anybody asks you why you changed them sheets, tell 'em you pissed in the bed. Shit, that ain't nothin' new. They'll believe it; you do it all the time."

He moved in closer to her and bent down to make his point clear. "Do you understand when I say you betta not say shit to nobody about this? 'Cause believe me, ain't nobody gon' believe you anyway. Hell, yo' momma don't even like you," he chuckled to himself.

"She tell me that shit all the time how she wish you was never born. And if you do tell anybody, she'll come ask me, and believe me, she'll take my side. Then she'll hate you even mo' fo' tryin' to break us up. Now hurry up, fo' them other lil' nosey bitches get home."

He stood up to fasten his wrinkled, dirty jeans and buckle up his belt. The look on his face no longer seemed affectionate to Dream. It was cold--dead almost--the same eyes she saw when her mother looked at her, un-loving and un-wanting.

Why would he say those things to me? I thought he loved me. That's what he told me when he brought me candy and toys. Just for me and not the others. When he bought me baby dolls and gave me a dollar for the bomb pop truck. Especially, when he said he wouldn't leave me, like my daddy did.

Ernest, Karen's drunken on-again, off-again boyfriend, was a trucker who only breezed through town every other weekend or so. Since Karen was never home when he arrived, she gave him keys to their fifth-floor project apartment.

Ernest baited Dream into his web of isolation over the preceding months with candy, dollar bills and toys. He knew she felt unloved and deserted by her family and he used that greatly to his advantage. He gave Dream things when no one was around so she would idolize him and feel special.

As with any molester, from the first moment he entered the apartment with Karen, he'd set his sights on his mark. Dream was always off to herself and always seemed withdrawn from the group. Once he got in good, found out what type of woman and mother Karen really was, he knew he was in. He soon began to set his plan in motion.

It was Dream's birthday, a day her family either forgot about or didn't care about. That day was the day Ernest decided to make his move. He had brought Dream a Betsy Wetsy Doll, the one she had begged for every time she'd seen it on the TV and wanted for months.

When Dream saw the doll, her heart filled with excitement and appreciation. When she jumped into his arms, Ernest told her to kiss him. Like any other day, Dream placed a soft child-like peck on his left cheek.

Ernest sat her down atop his lap and plotted out his every move. "That's not a good kiss for a gift you've been wanting for so long, now is it?"

Dream hunched her shoulders and replied, "I don't know."

"Well, I'll tell you. No, it's not. I had to go all over the city to find you that doll. Not to mention I'm the only one who cared enough to get you a present. You see, yo' momma 'nem don't give a damn about you. I think you should try that kiss again and really show some thankfulness."

Dream repeated the kiss on his cheek, harder this time.

"Now Dream, that was a little better but not good enough. You love me don't you?"

Dream nodded her head in compliance.

"Well, here then. Let me show you how you suppose to kiss a man you say you love."

Ernest opened Dream's mouth and forced his tongue inside with such a force, Dream gagged and began to choke.

"You not doin' it right. Now if you want me to continue to bring you nice presents and shit, you've gotta learn this, understand?"

Dream's feelings were hurt that she wasn't pleasing the only person that seemed to care for her besides her Nana Grace. She wanted him to keep being nice to her and would do anything to please him. She didn't want him to leave her behind like her daddy did.

"You gotta relax."

Dream closed her eyes tightly and like she'd seen her older sisters do many times with their boyfriends, she opened her mouth and tried to receive his kiss.

Ernest once again stuck his tongue inside her mouth. He leaned back and patted her on her back.

"Good, that was good, baby. Every time you see me from now on, that's how you kiss me—when no one is around of course. We don't want anyone to know about our special friendship, okay?"

Kisses turned to fondling, fondling to the jacking off of his penis, the jacking off of his penis to the splitting of the corners of her mouth as he shoved his over sized penis between her lips. That went on for what felt like forever to Dream. Her splitting lips finally led to blood between her thighs.

Dream slowly climbed down off the dingy white twin sized bed and began cleaning the room she shared with her sister, Vanessa, her legs almost buckling from the pain. She picked up her panties, blue jean shorts and her yellow Big Bird T-shirt from the floor and placed them in the Hefty trash bag they used for a dirty clothes hamper.

The pinkish colored liquid continued to ooze down her legs. She went into the bathroom and ran herself a bath. She returned to the bedroom and began removing the soiled linen from the heavily urine-stained mattress.

At only nine-years-old, Dream was smart enough to know that if someone found the sheets in the laundry, they would question her about the stains. So she balled up the sheets and placed them inside the kitchen trash can and made a mental note to empty the bin once she got out of the tub.

Dream went into the bathroom and stepped into the tub. The usual temperature she liked her bath water was unbearable to her. Her vagina hurt like hell and she could see the water turning colors. She sat on the ledge of the tub, let out some of the water and turned on the cold faucet to cool the water.

She went to replace the linen on her bed and returned to the tub. She was no longer crying outward, but inside she couldn't understand why Ernest was being so mean to her after she had given him what he wanted. The tears only began to fall as Dream thought back to what he'd said about her family and her mother, Karen's feelings towards her. She cried because she knew he was telling the truth. She had known it all along.

Karen would say things to her like, "Yo' damn daddy wasn't shit and you ain't gon' be shit just like him." Whether it was just wetting the bed or getting into trouble at school, Karen made sure she made her negative thoughts about her baby daughter known to her.

Dream sat in the water and soaked her swollen body parts as Ernest entered the bathroom with his keys in hand.

"Stop all that damn cryin'! Big girls don't cry. Now hush up and wash yo' ass."

Dream dried her face and began to wash up as she heard the front door to the apartment close.

A big girl? He said I'm a big girl? Doesn't he know, I'm only nine-years-old?

Dream got out of the tub and began to put on her clothes when she realized that her vagina was still leaking. She went into the closet, grabbed a washcloth, folded it into fours and placed it down between her thighs. Then she gathered her remaining items and returned to her room before anyone came home. She then climbed onto her bed and grabbed the doll Ernest had just given her for a birthday present. She hugged the doll with all her might.

It didn't matter to her that the pain inside her body was unbearable, all that mattered in Dream's nine-year-old mind was the doll Ernest had given her. The gift from him represented a symbol of affection and love in her eyes. And no matter how twisted, it was something Dream wasn't used to feeling inside that home.

Chapter Two

Ernest didn't hear the keys jingling in the front door at one A.M., in time to finish the deed. Karen wasn't due home from the strip club until three.

Ernest had come into Dream's bedroom that night, smelling strongly of Jack Daniels as he had done once a week over the past six years. From a young girl, through puberty, to a young woman, Ernest had stripped away both Dream's childhood and her self-worth.

Inside, she felt the confusion of a young girl's mind trying to live in an adult-framed world. She wanted to be loved by him. She felt no one else neither cared about her nor understood her. She thought that as long as she did what he asked her to do to please him, he would always be there. She could never have been more wrong.

Karen could hear the soft squeaking sound of Dream's twin sized bed, along with a male's voice moaning as she rounded the corner towards her own bedroom. Her older two girls were away for the weekend, so she knew it was her youngest daughter probably having sex with some young boy from the block.

Karen had already begun suspecting that Dream was having sex because of the way her body was forming and developing. Her baby daughter's breasts sat up high at 38C's and her ass and thighs had surpassed Karen's by the age of twelve.

As Karen reached over and flicked on the light to Dream's room, she almost fainted. There was Ernest, pounding away on her fifteen-year-old daughter in the world famous doggy-style position.

When he heard Dream gasp and noticed the horrified expression on her face, Ernest turned to find Karen standing in the doorway with her hands covering her mouth. He immediately pushed Dream down to the mattress and leaped off the bed towards Karen.

Karen was frozen in time. Her heart quickly became enraged, but not towards Ernest, it was unleashed bitterly towards Dream.

"You triflin' lil' slut!" she screamed as she lunged towards Dream on the bed.

Dream scurried to the top of the mattress and quickly covered herself with the navy blüe blanket.

Ernest shuffled to put on his clothes and begin trying to explain to Karen.

"Aey, baba…baby, it's not what you think! Wait! Calm down, let me explain."

Karen yanked Dream by the top of her head and dragged her out of the bed. Dream grabbed her mother's hands and tried to pry them a loose from her hair while kicking and screaming for her to stop and listen to her.

Karen unleashed a series of blows to Dreams face and head.

"I knew you were trouble! I knew yo' ass wasn't shit and I should've got rid of you a long fuckin' time ago. A wad of sperm that I should've let hit the fuckin' wall!"

Ernest pulled Karen from off the top of Dream and dragged her forcefully into the bedroom away from Dream.

When Dream heard the door slam, she scooted over to lock her bedroom door, put on some clothes and lay down on the floor to listen at the bottom of her door.

She knew Ernest would protect her. She knew he would straighten everything out with her mother. Yet, all she heard was Ernest apologizing for having too much to drink at Pop Shaw's Lounge and Dream coming into the living room with a T-shirt and no panties on. He lied and told Karen how Dream had flaunted her ass in front of him and bent down in front of the television as if she'd dropped something so he could see her pussy.

He even blamed Karen for always being gone when he came into town, and for working at the Pink Slip strip club over in East St. Louis.

Dream listened as he, the one person she thought loved her, manipulated her mother and turned her further against her daughter. He had simply added the match to the gasoline of hatred Karen had felt for her daughter for years.

Dream couldn't believe what she was hearing.

How could he say those things about me? It wasn't me who started this. All I did was try to please him. How can he say that shit about me? Why is he doing this to me?

Before Dream could reason within herself, Karen began to beat on her bedroom door, kicking it for Dream to open up and let her in. She wanted to hurt Dream for seducing the man she loved. She wanted to kill Dream as she reflected on both the joy and the pleasure in the sound of his voice, the sparkle she saw in his eyes once she hit the light switch and saw him fucking her.

Karen continued to punch the door with force. Dream withdrew to a corner opposite the end of the room, scared to death.

Finally it stopped, and Dream prayed it would all just go away but as she saw the knob on the door turn, she knew Karen had jimmied the lock with a knife.

Karen entered the room and stood in front of Dream with the blade in her hand.

"Why? Why you do this? Who taught you to be such a little slut that you would stoop this low and fuck my man? I work two fucking jobs to keep a roof over yo' head, clothes on yo' back, food in yo' stomach and this is how you fuckin' repay me? You nasty lil' bitch! You never wanted me to see me happy. Never wanted me to be around any man but yo' sorry ass daddy. Well get it through yo' fuckin' head, he dead! He ain't comin' back! He got his fuckin' head blown off, memba'?"

That sparked off rage inside Dream as she lunged at Karen with fury. Karen swung the knife to stop Dream mid-stride and promised Dream she'd take her life her without hesitation or a second thought.

"I bought yo' nasty ass in this world, I guarantee, you lil' hoe, I'll take you out!"

"But Momma, how you gon' believe him? He lyin'!"

"What he gotta lie fo'? You always have been the problem child. Always getting' into shit, stealin' from the store, lyin' all the time and pissin' all over the place and shit. How the fuck you gon' fuck somebody's man and still pissin' all over the fuckin' place?"

"Momma, please! You gotta believe me! I didn't do what he said I did! This ain't the first time we done this!"

Karen swung around and looked to Ernest in the doorway.

"She's a fuckin' lie!" he screamed, pointing his finger at Dream.

"You said it yo'self, baby, she lies all the damn time. Nothin' but a trouble maker, always tryin' to ruin yo' happiness."

"Trouble maker? Tell her how you used to bring me candy and give me money to kiss you. How you use to tell me you loved me while you made me touch you in certain places. Tell her!"

"Now that's a fuckin' lie too, baby!"

Dream looked back to Karen and pleaded with her to believe her.

"It's the truth Momma. It's been going on since I was nine years old."

Karen backhanded Dream and she fell to the floor.

"Liar! Just shut up! Shut up!"

Dream grabbed her face as the tears flowed.

Why won't she believe me? Damn, does she really love him that much or does she really just hate me that much?

Everybody was turning on her, making her look like the bad guy. Karen, she was used to. Ernest… she couldn't believe!

She looked up to her mother and continued to plead with her.

"Momma, please, you gotta believe me. He's been having sex with me since I was nine years old!" Dream screamed out.

"Say it one more time Dream and I swear I'll…"

"Momma, it's the truth!"

"Get out! Get up and get yo' hoe-ish ass out of my house, now!"

"*What?*" Dream whispered.

"Get out!"

"Momma, please don't..."

"I said, get the fuck out, Dream!"

Karen grabbed Dream by the arm and began to drag her out of the bedroom. Dream grabbed Karen's leg with her free arm and begged Karen to listen to her Dream sunk her nails in Karen's black fish net stockings.

Karen released her arm and reached down to grab both of Dream's legs and continued to drag her through the hallway, belly up.

Dreams eyes pleaded with Ernest to help her as he stood off to the side with a slight smirk on his face.

"Please, Ernest! Please help me! Please tell her! Why are you doing this to me? You said you loved me, please, help me…"

Karen unlocked the front door, snatched Dream by her shirt and pushed out the door. She locked the door behind her as Dream stood on the outside, half dressed, screaming and banging to get in.

Karen walked over to outstretched arms of Ernest and cried. Inside, she wanted, no… needed to believe Dream that was a liar. She couldn't bear to think, let alone except the reality of Dream's story. Couldn't imagine that type of horrible act going on all those years in her very own home underneath her very own nose. Therefore, the easiest thing to do, was to block it all out and the best way to do that was to get rid of the one thing that would always remind her of it; her daughter.

Chapter Three

Dream resigned from the door once it had become clear that Karen was not about to let her come back inside the apartment. She walked down the dirty, graffiti sprayed hallway to the elevator. The overwhelmingly strong odor of urine almost burned her nostrils as she waited for the elevator to reach the ground level.

Dream clutched her chest as she walked by all the local people still hanging out on the courtyard. She had almost made it across the parking lot of her Auntie's neighboring Peabody Projects parking lot when she saw them; crowd of young bucks, hanging out and shooting dice.

None of their faces looked familiar to her and Dream was afraid to walk by them. She sped up her pace but not fast enough to get by them unnoticed.

One of the young bangers called out to her as she passed them by. "Hey, Ma, what you doing out here this time of night? What you looking fo'? I got that heat fo' ya."

Dream responded by picking up her pace even faster and the young bangers responded by following her. As she heard the footsteps behind her get closer, She started running in fear for her life and kept running until she could run no more. One of the young bangers caught her by the shirt and yanked her down to the ground. One of his crewmembers grabbed both of Dreams legs and together they carried Dream behind a dumpster. She kicked and kicked at them as they tried to pry her legs apart but her efforts were to no avail.

It was a four-man conspiracy of rape, sexual battery and humiliation. As one took down her panties, one held her arms down onto the dirty ground, mixed with mud, drug needles, broken glass and trash. The third forced Dream's head towards his body and told her to open her mouth.

When she didn't comply, he punched Dream in her left jaw and continued to punish her until she obeyed.

The older one was already inside her, tearing away at her flesh, while this one was getting his satisfaction from her orally. The fourth culprit stood lookout as he patiently awaited his turn. Dream could hardly breathe, her jaw hurt like hell from his blows and the force at which he continuously shoved his penis in her mouth, made the pain that much more intense.

It seemed as though simultaneously, they unloaded their filth onto her body, the first inside her ailing vagina, the second disgracing her with his fluids all over her face. As his sperm mixed with Dream's tears, she silently wished they would just kill her, end the misery she had felt within her soul for so long.

After the other two took their prospective turns, Dream was left behind the dumpster, hunched over in pain and still bleeding from the inside of her now severely swollen jaw. She was lightheaded as she tried to stand to her feet. Her clothing was torn from top to bottom.

She stumbled across the dirt-filled pavement towards Dillion Street. All that was covering her bare chest were her arms, and her ripped up shorts were barely hiding her bottom.

When she reached the main street, she walked as fast as she could, given the pain, to try to reach the Mobile gas station a few blocks ahead. She was tired, more so emotionally than physically.

Just as she thought she could go no further, a black Monte Carlo pulled up beside her. At that moment, Dream was feeling so much despair, she didn't care if he wanted to go at her for round two. She wouldn't have even tried to fight back.

However, as the car came to a slow halt and the passenger side window descended, a middle-aged woman called out to her.

"Are you alright? Say, do you need some help?"

Dream ignored the woman and continued to stumble down the block. She was almost there but her legs alone could go no further. She stopped to address the woman in the driver's seat.

When Dream turned towards her and the woman saw the shadow of her face, she threw the car in park, jumped out and ran towards Dream. When she saw her up close, she wrapped her arms around her and allowed Dream to place her weight against her body.

"Who did this to you?" the woman asked.

"It doesn't matter," Dream whispered quietly.

"It does matter! Did your boyfriend do this to you?"

Dream didn't respond.

Boyfriend? Lady, you just don't know! You really don't wanna know. You wouldn't believe me if I told you anyway.

The woman escorted Dream to her car and formally introduced herself.

"My name is Dianna. What's your name?

"Dream."

"Dream? What a beautiful name."

Beautiful? Lady, you really trippin'. Nothin' about me is beautiful.

"Well Dream, do you think you can let me take you the hospital and get you looked at? You really need to see a doctor."

The woman opened her passenger side door and helped Dream inside. She went back to the trunk of the car to remove a sports jacket from inside. She gave Dream the jacket to cover herself, laced the seat belt around Dream's waist and closed the door. She walked around to the driver's side and entered the car.

"Dream, whoever did this to you, you didn't deserve it. No matter what they told you, how you feel right now or what anybody thinks. I'm so sorry this happened to you. Is there anyone I can call for you?"

Dream didn't even have to bust her brain on that one. No, there was no one she could call for her. No one who cared about her or her welfare, especially Karen.

If she did, she wouldn't have put me out the house at two a.m. in the first damn place.

Dianna took Dream to Cardinal Glennon Children's Hospital on Grand Avenue. When they entered the Emergency Room, Dianna walked Dream to the counter and asked for help.

As Dream sat in the examination room with her legs up in stirrups, she stared off at the ceiling. She was wishing her Nana were still alive.

She would help me, I know she would.

She bit down on her bottom lip as the doctor inserted the steel metal clamp into her bruised vagina and cried.

"Call the police and Social Services, now! There's massive tearing to the inside tissue," the doctor told the older female nurse.

"Who did this to you, young lady? Did you get a good look at him?"

When Dream didn't respond, the doctor resigned, finished her exam and walked up to Dream's bedside.

"Honey, I know you're scared. You have every right to be. But we are here to help you but we can't help you if you won't let us."

The only thing Dream could think about were the words Ernest had spoken to her: *"...And you betta not tell nobody. They won't believe you anyway. If you do, I'll never love you again…"*

Dream couldn't understand why that still mattered to her but in a strange way, it did. She couldn't stand the thought of going back to the days when absolutely no one loved her.

The elderly black doctor patted her on the thigh.

"It's okay. You don't have to tell me. We've called your mother, she's on the way."

Dream's heart lightened at the thought of Karen being worried about her and coming to get her. In Dream's mind, that must have meant that Karen had forgiven her but what Dream would soon find out was that "coming" sometimes, meant "going".

When Karen entered the room, Dream was asleep. Karen browsed over the room, the walls and everything else except her daughter. She didn't want to look at her; she couldn't look at her. Karen despised her for the turmoil she felt inside. She sat in the chair next to Dream's bed and waited for the doctor to come inside to speak with her.

"Mrs. Wilson, hello, I'm Dr. Carter. I was the attending physician when your daughter was brought in."

"Who bought her here?"

"A concerned woman was passing by on her way home from work. She saw her walking the streets in this condition and quickly brought her here to the ER. I'm sorry to have to tell you this but she's been brutally raped."

"Ump, so *you* say! I bet you any amount of money it didn't go down like that."

"Excuse me? Ms. Wilson, never in the years of my medical experience have I seen a young woman's vaginal tissue that torn and bruised from having consensual sex with someone."

"Look doctor, you don't know my child like I do," Karen said, raising her voice.

The elevation in her vocal cords caused Dream to awaken. The doctor, disgusted with Karen, rubbed Dream's lower calf.

"Well, I'm gonna leave you two alone to talk. And Dream, please think about what I said."

When the doctor left the room, Karen once again did her best to let the distaste she felt for her daughter be known.

"Look at you! You just simply live for making my life hell, don't you? Got me all up in this fuckin' hospital with these people looking at me like I'm crazy and shit. Look at yo' clothes, look how yo' fuckin' draws look! You are so fuckin' nasty... you... you just embarrassin', that's all."

Dream felt the tears fall once again. She had hoped that finally Karen was there to comfort her and take her home. But as she watched Karen walk to the door, purse in hand, she learned the hard way, she wasn't.

"Did you tell them *why* you was out there in the damn streets this time a night in the first damn place? I bet you didn't tell them how I caught yo' lil' nasty ass having sex with a grown ass man less than two fuckin' hours ago, did you?"

Karen waved her hand in the air.

"Well, guess what? I ain't finna be in and out no fuckin' courts with these white people all in up my business. You wanna be a hoe, be a hoe, but you won't be one under my damn roof! Let them take care of yo' ass from now on."

With that, she walked out and Dream felt the world settled down upon her shoulders. She picked up the remote from the stand next to her and turned on the TV. Since it was a children's hospital, the programming went off at eleven p.m. and so the only thing Dream could do was listen to the radio. Out came a song that told the story of her soul. The feelings that Dream as a child could not say nor understand. But as she lay there all alone, the music became a lullaby to her pain.

"...She faced the hardest times, you could imagine and many times, her eyes fought back the tears. And when her youthful world was about to fall in, each time her slender shoulders bore the weight of all her fears. And a sorrow no one hears, still rings in midnight silence, in her ears..."

Dream couldn't imagine someone else in the world knowing how she felt at that moment, but the song spoke to her soul.

"...Let her cry for she's a lady. Let her dream, for she is a child. Let the rain fall down upon her. She's a free and gentle flower, growing wild..."

Dream understood the words perfectly. And the fact that her name flowed freely in the song connected even more to her spirit. She didn't think she could hurt that intensely but she did. She grabbed the pillow and continued to cry. She cried and cried until she felt as if she cried her soul out, only she didn't even think anyone, even God cared enough to listen.

Chapter Four

Later that morning, around four a.m., the nurse came in to inform Dream that a representative from Child Welfare and the police department would be arriving shortly. Dream didn't want to go to foster care. She knew all too well what happened to young girls who got lost inside the system.

When the nurse left, Dream threw off the white cotton blanket, pulled her legs over the side of the mattress and struggled out of bed. She walked over to the door, checked both ways to see if anyone was watching and began her escape.

First, she pulled the tape off her skin, ripped the painful IV from her arm, gathered what was left of her clothing and quietly walked out of the room. She dipped into a nearby stairwell and slowly made her way down to the third floor. It was the L&D (Labor & Delivery) ward. She canvassed the hallway for one of the metal clothing bins. She wanted to steal a pair of scrubs.

She located the laundry hamper and found a pair of sky blue surgical scrubs. She went into the bathroom, slipped on the clothing, pocketed a few sanitary napkins and headed for the elevator.

She was hurting more inside than on the outside. She couldn't believe Karen could turn her back on her own flesh and blood like she did. Dream didn't know where she could to go or what she would do. When she reached the ground level, she went through the café' and out the door.

It was an overly warm early summer morning. As she slowly walked North on Grand Avenue, she finally came to rest at the intersection of Natural Bridge and Grand Avenue.

Fairground Park was one of the city's most visited parks and as Dream looked around at all of it patron's, she felt a little more comfortable in the crowded environment.

She walked over to the swimming pool and watched as the neighborhood kids played in the water.

From across the pool area, he noticed her. It was as if he could sense the weakness in her… the need in her. He walked over to her and pointed to the seat beside her.

"Damn, pretty girl, can I keep you company?"

Dream looked up and couldn't believe her eyes. He was fine! His skin was caramel brown, his eyelashes long and thick, his hair styled in a long Jerry Curl and his body stacked tight with muscles. He was wearing nothing but a pair of Nike basketball shorts and a pair of Nike tennis. She was fascinated by the gold on his hands, on his wrists and around his neck.

"Why would you wanna sit by me?" she asked, trying to cover the bruises on her face.

"'Cause it looks to me, like you could use a friend," he said, extending his hand to her. "I'm Pieces and you are?"

Dream placed her hand inside his but kept her eyes to the ground.

"Dream."

"Dream. That name fits you. You look like a dream."

Dream wondered how she could sit and even entertain the thought of talking to a man. But sad to say, it was the only thing she had come to know.

"I see you checking out all this bling I got on. Nice huh? You like nice things, Dream?"

Dream thought for a moment and shook her head.

"I can help you get nice things. All the nice things that young girls your age can't afford."

"Really? How?" Dream questioned, her eyes still focused on the concrete below her.

"Easy. It's what I do. I make new friends, young and beautiful friends such as yo'self, and I buy 'em nice things, take care of their every need. I also protect 'em," he said, pulling Dream's face towards him. "And from the looks of it, you definitely can use my protection."

Dream let her face fall to the ground.

"Why do you do all that? What you get out of it?"

"Well, it's kinda like a mutual friendship. I take care of you and you do little things for me when I ask you to. Now that don't sound too hard now, do it? And a young tender such as yo'self, I know we can make each other real happy. Wouldn't you like to be happy, Dream?"

Would she? She couldn't remember too many happy times in her life after her dad had passed away. She thought she'd found it in Ernest but he proved her to be dead wrong.

"Where do you live?" he asked Dream.

"No where."

Pieces smiled to himself.

Yeah, I knew I picked a good one. Ain't got shit and need every thang. These be the best ones, the dependent ones and the desperate ones make the best hoes.

"I got a lil' sister I want you to meet. She lives with me down on Washington and Sarah. If ya'll hit it off, you can come and stay with us. We got an extra bedroom. I just want you to meet her. Is that alright with you?"

Dream shook her head as Pieces called the young woman out of the pool and over to them.

Ebony was a sixteen-year-old runaway who left her grandmother's house two years earlier. Like Dream, Ebony had experienced abuse on every level at the hands of her brothers and uncles. Her blind, elderly grandmother could do nothing to protect her from the predators she claimed as family. Ebony left for school one morning and never returned. She met Pieces on the way to Steven's Middle School and just as he did Dream, he promised her nice things and protection in exchange for favors.

Ebony didn't mind the treacherous and constant use of her body for money. She liked being the envy of all the young neighborhood girls, like the way they stared at her when Pieces picked her up from places and dropped her off in his nice car. She liked being able to buy whatever she wanted, when she wanted.

The money got so good to her and Pieces, that he labeled her his star and formed a partnership with Ebony to recruit other young and helpless girls--girls like Dream, with low self-esteem, a broken home, or those looking for love in all the wrong places. These were the ones he could easily control and fuck with, mentally.

As Ebony approached and Pieces walked away, Dream called after him, "Thanks!"

Pieces whispered in Ebony's ear, "She's a good catch. Reel that lil' bitch in."

Ebony shook her head in agreement and smiled. Pieces then turned to acknowledge Dream's remark.

"No problem, baby girl."

You'll be thankin' me the rest of yo' life, he muttered to himself.

Ebony extended her hand to Dream as she took the seat beside her on the bench.

"Hi, I'm Ebony," she said as she stroked Dreams ponytail. "You got some pretty hair. You're a pretty girl."

"Thanks," Dream answered, eyes still glued to the ground.

Ebony looked at Dream's face.

"So what's yo' story, ma? Crazy boyfriend? Drunk ass daddy?"

Dream hunched her shoulders.

"Girl, my face use to look like that sometimes too, so don't feel bad. Only, it was my uncle who used to beat me if I didn't give him want he wanted."

Dream looked to her.

"Oh yeah, he use to be so nice to me when me and my two brothers first moved in with him, my other uncle and my grandma. Used to dog my brothers out after they took us from our momma but he was always so nice to me. Then he started touchin' me in places I knew he didn't have no business doing so. It got so bad in that house, I ended up havin' a baby by one of 'em; my uncle, my other uncle or my brother…I just didn't know."

"Where's your baby?" Dream asked.

"I gave it away. Never laid eyes on it; don't even know what it was. I mean really, why would I want another me in the world? Just another person some sick bastard would hurt anyway."

Dream's eyes watered as she thought of how Ebony must have felt. She only had one monster to deal with. She couldn't imagine three.

"But then I met Pieces," Ebony continued. "He took care of that situation for me and never let me look back. He takes really good care of me too. Makes me the envy of all the lil' skeezers round here. And he'll do the same for you. He's just good like that. I know some people say he's not a good person, but I disagree. He's been nothin' but good to me," she lied.

There had been many times Ebony had suffered a beating at the hands of Pieces for reasons she wanted to keep private. Dream, Ebony figured, would find out soon enough on her own.

"So, what do you say?"

Dream connected with her instantly. She felt her pain and Dream was sure that Ebony would be the one to really understand her from that point on.

"I'll go."

"Good! Let's go let Pieces know the good news. We have a new sister."

Dream smiled at the thought of being apart of something… a family. When the girls reached Pieces, he looked to Dream.

"So, pretty girl, you gon' join us or what?"

"She sure is," Ebony said, winking her eye at Pieces.

Pieces reached in his pocket and pulled out a wad of cash. He removed a twenty-dollar bill from the stack of green and handed it to Dream.

"Dream, why don't you go buy yo'self somethin' from the stand over there. We'll be ready to leave in a few."

"Thank you," she said again. She was starving. She hadn't stayed around and waited on breakfast at the hospital.

"It's nothing. Only the beginning."

When Dream was out of range, Pieces kissed Ebony on the forehead.

"Good job," he told her.

"You know it," she replied.

Chapter Five

When Dream entered the house with Pieces and Ebony, she was impressed. The living room was decked out in black and beige. The sofa and love seat were black leather with beige leather throw pillows. The table set was made of beige wood and smoked mirrors. The walls were nicely lined with black art. The all-black entertainment center held a 47 inch color TV and a nice Panasonic stereo system.

To look around, you would have never known she was standing in a full fledged "whore house." It was clean, smelled fresh and looked as if it were your typical family home. But Dream was about to find out that having things like this came at a price and to even lay her head there, was gonna cost her.

When Ebony opened the door to Dream's bedroom, Dream's stomach tied up in knots. It was dark and dingy. In one corner was an old broken down twin-sized bed. No cover was on the stained mattress, no pretty pictures were on the wall, no curtains were on the window and the walls were filthy. Dream looked down at the heavily stained carpet and frowned. It looked as if it were old blood smeared across the floor.

Ebony touched her on the shoulder and told her she was glad Dream decided to come and stay with them. At that moment, Dream wasn't so sure she had made the right decision. Yet, she also realized she didn't have much of a choice.

It beats sleeping in the park or in some vacant house.

Dream smiled. "Thanks for letting me stay."

"Come on, I'll show you my room."

Dream couldn't wait to see what was behind "door number two". When Ebony unlocked the padlock on her door and pushed it open, Dream's mouth almost hit the floor. Ebony's room was the same as the front room--beautiful.

Burgundy satin sheets were on her black, steel canopy bed. Matching curtains set the stage for a room full of erotica. Lining the walls were pictures of Ebony herself and tons of diamond-shaped mirrors. There was a plush burgundy rug on the floor and a 30-inch TV sitting on top of an pretty nice oak dresser.

"Your room looks really nice, Ebony. And look at all these clothes in your closet. All these shoes. Man, I bet you go outside fly everyday. My momma would've never buy me things like this. She was too busy shoppin' at the thrift stores, then sendin' all the hand-me-downs to me. I see why you say all the girls be jealous of you. You got some fly stuff in here."

It was all part of the plan for Ebony and Pieces. They would bring a young girl such as Dream to their home; show them all the things they could have by joining their family and then send them to the room Dream had been given. By nature, they're gonna always want the things Ebony has and by nature, they're gonna do what they have to do to get it.

Ebony could tell Dream was one of those girls by the way she seemed to be in awe of the things Ebony had. Ebony smiled.

"Pieces made all these things possible for me and he's gonna do the same for you. Remember those little favors he was talking about? Well, it's those favors that got me all this stuff and this..."

She walked over to her bed and lifted the top end of the mattress. From under the mattress, Ebony pulled out a stack of money. It was one of their newest additions to the game. Ebony had taken two twenty-dollar bills and placed one on each side of a neatly cut stack of white paper, to make it look like she had a fat stack of cash. The response was always the same.

"Man, where you get all that money?"

Ebony smiled at Dream and nodded her head towards the living room. Dream turned to see Pieces sitting on the couch, counting out his cash as well. The sight of the money damn near made Dream's mouth water and like clockwork, she fell into their trap, hook, line and sinker.

"What do I have to do to make money like that? I mean what kind of favors do I have to do for him?"

"It's nothin' really," she lied. "Every now and then Pieces has these friends that like to spend large amounts of money with him. In return, Pieces like for me and a few of my friends to keep them company. For that, he keeps me laced with all this."

"That's all? Just keep someone company from time to time?"

"Yep, that's it. But you don't have to worry about all that right now. Let's get your room cleaned up for you first."

Dream followed Ebony into the hallway as she reached into the closet and pulled out a set of stained grey bed sheets that looked as if they used to be white at one point. Ebony noticed the look on Dream's face as she glanced at the sheets in Ebony's hand and then back to the one's on Ebony's bed.

Ebony couldn't help but chuckle at the fact that Dream fit right into the program. Ebony threw the old sheets on the floor, walked into her bedroom, opened her bottom drawer and pulled out a set of black satin bed sheets. From the smile Dream now possessed, Ebony knew that she was pleased.

"Here, you can have these."

"Thanks Ebony, that's really nice of you."

Dream walked into her new bedroom and simply couldn't believe that this room was a part of the rest of the house. Ebony soon entered with a white bucket, Pine Sol, a rag, a broom and a dust mop.

Dream began wiping the walls first and immediately could tell the difference in color. She scrubbed until her arms were tired. By the time she was done cleaning the walls, wiping down the old dusty brown furniture and bed rails, making the bed and sweeping the floor, the room was acceptable.

She was actually a little excited about having her own room. She had always shared a room with her next oldest sister, Vanessa. Now, she had her own space and it felt nice.

But I want a room like Ebony's. I want the pretty clothes, the nice shoes and that fat money stack like the one under her mattress. I wanna be the envy of the girls in the 'hood too.

Too naive to realize the price she had to pay to accomplish these things, Dream sat in the tub of a bubble bath and allowed herself to picture her world in the fast lane, filled with jewelry, money, cars and clothes.

Ebony had brought her a set of cozy pajamas, some candles and music to make her bath complete. The hot water, while soothing to her muscles, burned her bruises like hell, especially, the ones between her thighs.

Her mind drifted back to the first time it hurt her to take a bath, the pain she felt, both mentally and physically, the confusion and the disappointment. A tear rolled down the side of her cheek and Dream still could not understand why the people that said they loved her, were the ones who had hurt her so much and then literally disowned her. They tossed her away like the end pieces of a bad loaf of bread.

The music on the radio had spoken her feelings. It had voiced her emotions in a way she had never felt nor understood. It was as if the voice on the radio was inside her heart. The words were telling the story of her soul over a soft melody.

"...Since you been away, I've been down and lonely. Since you been away, I've been thinking of you. Tryin' to understand the reason you left me. What were going through? Oooooh, I'm missing you. Tell me where the road turns..."

As the sweat from the steam coming off the water mixed with her tears, Dream wiped her faced with washcloth and tried to pull herself together.

This is my life and I have to deal with it, no matter what. But damn, why it gotta hurt so bad?

Ebony went into the living room and sat down on the couch beside Pieces. He rubbed her head and smiled.

"You know we make a good team, don't you?"

"Yeah, I know."

"You did real good today bringin' this one in. She gon' make us a lot of money." He reached on the coffee table and handed Ebony two, one-hundred-dollar bills.

"Finder's fee," he chuckled.

Ebony folded the money, placed it inside her bra and stared down at the floor. She felt bad sometimes for the way he used her but Pieces was all she had in the world and he knew that. Ebony couldn't thank him enough for getting her away from the house of horror she went home to every day. He took her in and gave her a place to stay, and although she paid a high price for the roof over her head, she was grateful not to be sleeping under the Adelaide Bridge anymore.

The memories were often to painful to recall. The chill of the night still made her cry sometimes. His face, still appearing in her dreams off and on. The smell from his body, gross enough to make her throw up. The rough, rugged hair on his face felt as if it was slicing her face as he continuously tried to force his tongue down her throat.

She had grown tired of sleeping with layers of clothing on night after night. They took turns it seemed, on certain nights of the week. Her blood, her family… her nightmare.

Ebony had decided not to go home after school one day and walked aimlessly until her feet could go no more. She had three dollars and forty-eight cents in her pocket. She stopped at the Chop Suey on St. Louis Ave at 21st Street, got her a half order of beef fried rice and continued to walk until she finally came to rest under the Adelaide St. Bridge next to the train tracks.

She was tired and she was cold, but facing the weather outside was a better option than facing what would happen in her own bed, if she went home that night.

It was Friday night, which meant that her uncles would be drinking, and when they were drunk, their pleasure became her pain.

Ebony had heard that a lot of runaway girls slept under the bridge until they could find better shelter or someone to take them in, but this night the strip was virtually empty.

She ate her rice, found a broken down box and laid it underneath one of the few spots that was well lit. She curled up on the cardboard in a fetal position and tried her best to keep warm. She was scared as hell but she honestly didn't think that anything could be worse than going back to that hellhole. That thought couldn't have been further from the truth.

His forceful touch startled her. The grabbing at her legs was unwelcomed. Yet, he was determined to get his rocks off with the fifteen-year-old girl. He dropped his body weight on top of her and gripped her around her chin. She tried to jerk her head away, sharply from his grip but he had her chin pressed tightly between his fingers.

"Shhh! Now you hush yo' pretty lil' mouth and I'm not gon' hurt you."

Ebony squirmed and tried to force him from on top of her. She tugged at his filthy shirt and tried to pry her knee between his legs but he was simply to strong for her.

"I said be still and this'll all be over soon. Stop fightin' it!"

The first series of slaps hit her hard across her cheek and Ebony resigned. She just bit down on her bottom lip and let him finish his business. She lay there on the verge of breaking down and wondered if all men in the world were like the ones she'd come across... her uncles and even her own brother.

Her present day answer came as Pieces pushed her head down towards his awaiting piece of meat and nodded for her to put her mouth around it. It didn't really matter how much money she made him or how many girls she brought for him to turn out. To Pieces, Ebony was just another hoe.

Chapter Six

Over the next few days, Pieces allowed Dream to rest up and Ebony to take a few days off to keep her company. But he had begun to grow impatient and was now ready for his new moneymaker to hit the streets.

He had given Ebony five hundred dollars to go and buy Dream some clothes a few days before. He had paid to get her hair done earlier that day at *The Drop Shop* and now it was Dream's turn, to return the favor.

Dream was lying on the bed, listening to music when Ebony came inside.

"Hey girl, what you up to?"

"Nothin' much. Just laying here listening to the radio."

Dream sat up on the bed.

"Ebony, you ever trip off how music seems to relate to all your problems? How the DJ seems to know what you goin' through before he hits the air waves?"

"Yeah, crazy huh?" Ebony replied. "I just figure it's 'cause, you know, everybody go through shit. Some people's shit is just different. My momma's shit was crack. Overdosed one day right in front of me and my two brothers. Laid there in front of me, white shit oozin' out the side of her mouth, eyes wide open, gazin' up at the ceiling as if she was amazed at what she saw. Got a bad batch of dope and left us here by ourselves."

Ebony stared off at the ceiling.

"Left us here to live in hell," she mumbled. Ebony turned to look at Dream. "Everybody got they own shit to deal with Dream, they own story to write."

"Yeah, I guess so. But do you really think that rich people like the singers and actors on TV have the same problems we do? I mean, they rich! Money should make they lives hella easy, don't you think?"

Ebony smirked. "Naw, they just better at hidin' they shit from the world. They able to express it in different ways. Just listen..."

Dream leaned back against the pillow and focused on the pain she heard flowing through the speakers of the radio.

"...But deep down inside of me, my heart is empty. Girl can't you see? Sometimes I'm low in despair, with no one to care. Please love, don't leave me there. I'm so all alone, I have no one to call my own. And when I'm weak, there's no one there, to make me strong. I am searchin' for love, searchin' for love..."

"See what I'm sayin'? Even the rich and famous has problems with the people around them. You can have all the money in the world and still be the loneliest person in the world, Dream. You'll never know who is really there because they genuinely care about you. You'll always wonder what it is they really want from you.

People *always* have ulterior motives for wanting to be in your life, Dream. You might as well learn that right now, right here, at this very moment in yo' life. Everybody wants somethin' from you. Nothin' is free, you hear me? Nothin' in this life is given to you without the expectation of somethin' in return."

Dream sat back and thought of Ernest and how he baited her into his sick and twisted world with toys, gifts and money.

She's so right.

"Especially from niggas and in some instances, bitches too. I say that to say, do what you gotta do to survive out here, Dream. Yo' family don't love you, fuck 'em! Yo' so-called friends turn they back on you, fuck them too! Because the harsh reality is, don't nobody owe you shit in this life. You gotta get out here and make it the best way you know how, by any means necessary. You take that to yo' grave.

Trust me, Dream, I ain't tellin' you somethin' I saw on TV or read in some book. This was shit I had to learn the hard way. But my granny always said that some of life's best lessons were the ones you had to learn the hard way 'cause they stay with you longer. You remember that."

Ebony hit Dream on the leg and rose up off the bed.

"Well, get some rest. I'm sure you could use it and you're definitely gonna need it."

Dream plopped back onto the bed. She called after Ebony and asked her what she needed to rest for.

"Don't trip off of it tonight. We'll talk about it tomorrow."

When Ebony exited Dream's room and rounded the corner, she ran right into Pieces.

"She ready yet? I done let her rest long enough. It's time to get this paper, Eb. I want her on the stroll with you tomorrow night, got it?"

"I got it," Ebony replied as she closed her door to her room.

Pieces could sense that Ebony's thoughts about Dream were different from the other girls they had previously had in the house with them.

Ebony felt bad for Dream. She understood her pain, she just didn't know how to reach out to her in the way Dream needed her too. The only thing Ebony could do was to put her up on the game, teach her all she knew about the streets and make her strong enough to handle whatever might come her way.

Ebony lay in the bed and thought back to her first night on the stroll. How scared she was, how nasty and dirty she felt, how the various parts of her body and jaws had hurt like hell the following morning. She knew that Dream would experience the same thoughts and emotions but it wasn't her place to detour Dream in another direction.

Ebony was loyal to Pieces and she couldn't allow that to change. She owed him too much and refused to live in fear of the repercussions she would face if she told Dream what Pieces really had planned for her. So she closed her eyes, clutched her pillow and resigned to the fact that if she couldn't save Dream *from* the stroll, she could teach her how to be the best hoe *on* the stroll.

Chapter Seven

The next evening, Ebony dressed Dream in her one of her most popular outfits, a midnight blue striped mini skirt with ruffles around the bottom and a matching halter-top. She gave Dream a pair of her newest white sandals that strapped up around her calves, made up her face with pretty colors and spiked up her hair in the air.

Dream had never felt so pretty and Ebony knew it from the smile on her face. She turned to Ebony.

"Thanks Ebony. I didn't know I could look like this! You got me lookin' like a model or somethin'! Where we goin'?"

"Well, you remember those favors I told you Pieces asked us to do for him sometimes? Well, now you about to find out what I was talkin' about. We about to go make some money. You know, keep a few guys company and shit, that's all."

Ebony could sense the uneasiness in Dream's face.

"Come on, let's go show Pieces the new you."

Dream followed Ebony into the living room where Pieces was waiting for them on the couch. When he saw Dream his eyes no longer saw her as the young helpless girl in the park. She became an instant moneymaker, a top of the line hoe and he intended to get full use of her, not only that night but for many nights to come.

"Damn, baby girl! You shol' lookin' good! My friends out there on the streets gon' love the shit out of you!"

He looked to Ebony as he rose up off the couch and walked over to Dream.

"You did a good job, Eb. Shit, I got a good mind to keep her to myself."

Unbeknownst to Dream, the meaning behind the compliment, she felt good that Pieces thought she was pretty enough to be his girl.

Ebony, on the other hand, wanted to spit in his face.

Ain't that a bitch! Now he wanna use her up like he did me? I'm top bitch in this house!

Pieces walked over to the door and ignored the look on Ebony's face.

"Ya'll ready to do this? You ready, Dream? You ready to make me a very happy man?"

Dream naively smiled and shook her head.

"Well, let's make it happen," he said, looking to Ebony.

Pieces escorted the girls out onto the front porch and took a seat on the ledge.

"Ebony can take it from here. I'll be right here, watchin'."

Watchin'? Dream asked herself. *Watchin' what?*

Ebony grabbed Dream by the arm.

"Come on, Dream, let's get out of here."

Ebony walked Dream down to the corner of Vander Venter and Washington Avenue and turned to look back at Pieces. He gestured with his hands for them to keep moving.

Ebony turned to Dream.

"Look, it ain't no use in tryin' to sugar coat nothin' for you no mo'. Remember last night when I told you that you had to get out here and survive by any means necessary? Well, that time is here. The company we about to keep, is waiting for us across the street over there."

Dream looked across the street, dumbfounded.

"Where? I don't see nobody. All I see is them girls getting' into them cars over there."

"Exactly! That's how we keep his friends company. They pay us to hang out with them for while. We in turn pay

Pieces his percent for watchin' out for us and makin' sure none of his friends try to hurt us in the process."

"So what are we supposed to do with them?"

"Come on Dream, are you really that naive or just plain stupid? We keep 'em company. Whatever that means. For some, it requires talkin', for some it takes kissin' them on they dick and for some it means they want some pussy or both."

"What?" Dream said almost in a whisper. "You mean we gotta have sex with 'em? I ain't finna have sex with them men! I don't know them! No! I ain't gon' do it! Take me back to the house."

"You think this a game he playin'? Look back at him. What is he doin'?"

Dream looked over to see Pieces standing on the top step with his gun in his waist and lookin' down at his watch.

Why didn't I see that gun a minute ago?

"Time is money, Eb. Get movin'!"

Dream looked back to Ebony, horrified. Ebony looked down at the ground.

"Look, Dream. You here now. When he found you in the park, you had nothin'. Nothin' to eat, not a stitch of clothes and no where to lay yo' head. He ain't gon' let you forget that. Now you say you want the things I have, well here we are. This is how I get 'em. You owe him now, just like I did. So you might as well suck it up and grow up. 'Cause if you don't, somebody's gonna really hurt you out here in these streets, namely him," she said, nodding back towards Pieces.

"But..."

"No buts. It is what it is, Dream. What you saving yo' self for, marriage? Love?" she chuckled.

"Shit, we already been robbed of that Princess shit long time ago. The one with the white picket fence, a dog, three kids and Prince Charming. The beauty of it was already stolen from us by these bastards, and all they left us with was tears and nightmares. So now it's time to say fuck that shit and know that if a man ever wants to get between yo' legs again, especially against yo' will, then you gotta make him pay for it. Don't walk away from it being the only one that feels used. You get what you can get and keep getting' it until you can have all the real shit you want in life.

Now you have two choices, Dream: You can walk with me, ride with me and learn the ropes to this game or you can turn around and go tell Pieces that this ain't what you wanna do. Tell him fuck 'em for takin' you in, fuck 'em for putting clothes on yo' back and shoes on yo' feet. But look at me, Dream. Look at me!"

Dream lifted her head to face Ebony.

"You don't wanna do that," Ebony told her, shaking her head.

For the first time, Dream saw fear in Ebony's eyes and it was then that she knew this was not a dream, it was real. Dream sighed as she felt a tear roll down her cheek.

"He's not yo' brother, is he?" Dream asked her.

Ebony just looked off to the cars approaching across the street.

"Come on, let's go."

Ebony led Dream across VanderVenter Avenue to an empty parking lot next to an old abandoned church.

"This is the corner I usually work. Here's how it works: Our customers, well, our tricks pull up..."

"Tricks?"

"Yeah, we call 'em tricks because they just some niggas trickin' off they pay checks on a piece of pussy. Anyway, they pull up, I ask 'em what they checkin' fo', they'll either say, 'I want some dome or the tunnel'. The dome means they want a blow job. The tunnel means they want some ass.

Some will say they wanna go round the world. That means they want it all, and fo' that they must pay, dearly. On a good night, I pull in eight to nine-hundred dollars. Pieces take half of whatever you make as his pay for protection. Even so, that leaves me with enough money to do me.

Most of these girls out here, got habits they gotta feed, dope and shit like that. Don't get into that shit, Dream, 'cause you'll end up out here hoein' just fo' the sake of shootin' up or smokin' crack. You gotta be strong to handle this shit out here and you gotta be smart.

I'm a let you ride with me on the first one, but hell, it ain't like you ain't never been fucked before. So, after that, you on yo' own."

Dream felt queasy standing in front of the vacant building, watching the girls jump in and out of cars.

They seem as if they ain't even phased by it.

A car pulled up next to them, and inside was a frail looking, fifty-plus-year-old man. His hairline was receding halfway back towards his neck. He pressed the down button on the automatic window and smiled.

"Hey there, pretty girl!"

Ebony smiled and looked to Dream.

"You're in luck. He's one of my regulars. He's pretty much harmless. Come on, get in."

Dream climbed in the back seat and listened in as Ebony and her client chitchatted as if they were old friends.

"Pull around the corner."

The car came to rest on the corner of Sarah and Washington Avenue as Ebony reached over, unzipped the man's checkered shorts and removed his pinkie-sized jimmy from his underwear. She began to stroke it while looking back at Dream. She gave her a wink.

Dream almost chuckled at the sight of his childlike jimmy. Even more amusing to her was the way he reacted to

Ebony's touch. It was as if he was about to explode on contact.

"By the way, Steve, this is my friend, Dream. Dream, this is Steve."

The man was moaning so loudly, he couldn't hear a word being said to him.

Ebony gestured for Steve to turn around and look at Dream. Then she instructed Dream to lift up her shirt and show him her breasts.

Dream looked at Ebony like she had just asked her to jump off a bridge. Ebony, in return, reminded Dream what the game was all about.

"You wanna get paid or what?"

Dream hesitated, but as the man grew more and more excited by Ebony's lips, which were now wrapped around what little jimmy he had. Dream joined in on the activity.

Steve got so turned on at the sight of Dreams young, maturing 38C breasts, he almost passed out.

"Lean up here, sweet thang. Let me touch 'em. I'll put a lil' somethin' extra in it for you. Just let me touch 'em."

Dream scooted up to the edge of the rear seat and allowed the old pervert to play with her nipples while Ebony jacked him off in the front seat.

Dream had never seen a man actually squirt out his cum all over himself before, but as his hands clenched down on her breasts, he looked as if he was convulsing as Ebony jacked him off with her hand.

When his blood pressure returned to normal, Ebony used his towel to wipe him off, along with her hand. He reached in his back pocket of his shorts and pulled out his little black wallet. He handed Ebony a crisp one-hundred-dollar bill. Then he smiled at Dream as he handed her two twenty-dollar-bills.

Damn, forty dollars just for lettin' him play with my titties! Ebony was right; men will pay to use you.

When they got back around the corner to the stroll, Ebony glanced over at Dream.

"Not bad, huh?"

Dream hunched her shoulders.

"Look, it's what you make it. Detach yo'self from it, that way it won't be nothing personal to you, just business. Now, you think you can handle it?"

Dream was both unsure and afraid. She had never had sex voluntarily before. All of her experiences were forced upon her in some sort of way.

"Just make sure they got rubbers. If not, make sure *you* got yo' own. Don't fuck nobody, without a rubber. It's some drastic shit goin on out here. Got it? And I don't give a fuck how much he payin', never let a nigga buss a nut in yo' mouth, Don't make no sense to protect yo' pussy from the disease and then swallow the shit, got it?"

Dream shook her head and waited with Ebony until the next car rolled around the corner. Within minutes, Dream was off on her own, using her body, among other things to find her way in the world. She sold her lips, her hips and her soul; only by the end of the night, it no longer mattered.

Dream had made $750, the most she had ever held inside her hand at one time. Pieces divided the money on the table down the middle and smirked to himself.

"Not bad fo' the first night, baby. Not bad at all."

Dream went into the bathroom, turned on the shower, grabbed a washcloth and a bar of soap. She scrubbed and scrubbed until it felt as if she'd scrubbed the skin right off her body. She wanted to rid herself of their smell, their touch, their taste and their juices.

She let the tears flow. She felt just as Ebony had said; dirty, used and abused. But Ebony was right in Dream's eyes. Men had tarnished her childhood. They had stolen her innocence and stripped her of her youth.

Dream had given way to the thoughts of how easy it was to make that kind of money in such a little time. She had made an instant decision that if a man wanted to continue to try to use her for his pleasure, then like Ebony had schooled her, she would make them pay.

No longer would they be the only ones to walk away with the sense that they had robbed her of something for nothing. No longer would they capitalize off her shame, profit from her unhappiness or take away that which was supposed to be invaluable and pay nothing. No longer would it happen, because that night…that night, Dream was inaugurated a hoe!

Chapter Eight

Dream learned the basic rules to hoeing and learned them well.

One: Always see the money first.

Two: Keep all tricks that's paying under $50 to a fifteen-minute maximum. That freed you up to always be available to make that real paper. To accomplish this, Dream learned to squeeze the muscles in her vagina, grip his penis and force him to cum.

Three: Never lie flat on your back. It was safer to serve them doggie style in case you have to move quickly and get away.

Four: Never jump in a car with a new trick. Always have him meet you on your turf until he becomes a regular.

Dream tried her best to live and die by these rules of the hoe stroll but there were mistakes and consequences along the way.

Two years later after turning her first trick, Dream gave birth to a seven-pound baby girl, born out of prostitution. She had continued to work the streets throughout her pregnancy and the thought of a baby growing inside her made Dream's thirst for money grow even further. Compared to the money she was giving Pieces, she was bringing in chicken scratch. If she made a thousand dollars, Pieces took five hundred of that, and now she'd have another mouth to feed. For that reason, Dream worked the streets up until the night her water broke.

When she held her newborn daughter in her arms for the first time, she finally felt she had something of her own to love. And unlike Ebony, she couldn't imagine being without her new baby girl.

I promise you on my life, I'll never let anybody hurt you. I'll always be there to love and protect you. You'll never know what it feels like to have yo' body used and abused.

Dream knew she'd do anything she had to do to take care of her baby and keep her safe. She wouldn't allow anyone to hurt her. Nobody, unlike her mother, Karen.

Although she felt that nuturing love for her newborn child, Dream also had to face reality. She wasn't able to financially care for her at that moment, and above all, she wanted her to be somewhere safe, somewhere stable until she could get herself together. With tears in her eyes, Dream tearfully decided her baby would be better off somewhere else for a while, preferably, with one of her sisters. They all were older than she was and caring for children of their own. Yet, the one she was closest to was still living at home with her mother.

Dream prayed her sister Lynnette would take her baby in and allow Dream to bring money by on a daily basis to take care of all her needs. That way, Dream could work the streets overtime, stack her money and save up enough to leave the hoe stroll for good.

She hadn't talked to them in years. Dream had seen her older two sisters on the streets, but they just turned their noses up at her and acted as if the mere sight of her, disgusted them. Yet inside, Dream figured her daughter was innocent; blood of their blood and even though they didn't deal with Dream herself, she prayed that maybe it would be different for her daughter.

Dream picked up the phone and dialed the familiar number to Karen's project apartment. She couldn't understand why Karen hadn't left the ghetto yet. She was sure that Karen was making a decent living now that she had finished Pharmacy Tech School. She guessed Karen was just like that, 'hood rat to the bone.

Karen's voice came over the receiver and Dream's heart instantly felt confused. A part of her was happy to hear her mother's voice. She hadn't heard it since that night at the hospital. The other side wanted to hate her for turning her back on her when she needed her the most.

"Momma," Dream whispered.

"Who is this?" Karen snapped. She knew it was Dream.

"It's me, Momma, Dream."

The line fell silent.

"I had a baby, Momma, a girl. Just had her this mornin'. She's seven pounds, eight ounces and she has a head full of hair."

Still, there was no response from Karen. She too was torn on the other end of the line. She often wondered what was happening to Dream out there in the streets. She had often heard stories from her daughters and friends about seeing her baby daughter out on the stroll. But the guilt of her failure as a mother was an emotion Karen wasn't emotionally and mentally able to handle. It was easier as usual for her to turn her away...and she did.

"Momma, you there?"

"What you callin' me fo', Dream? I washed my fuckin' hands of you a long time ago," Karen, responded with nothing but pure funk and resentment in her voice.

"Well, I was wonderin', I mean, I know you won't let me come back home... but I was kinda wonderin' if my baby could come and stay with you and..."

"Dream, you can stop yo' sentence right there. Not only are you not welcomed in my house again but I don't want no part of you here either! What you thought, I was gon' raise *another* lil' slut in my house? No thank you. Keep that problem yo'self. Maybe you'll see how it feels!"

"But Momma..."

"Click!"

Karen slammed down the phone to emphasize her point as Dream let the tears flow. She looked down to the tiny infant resting on her chest and whispered to her, "Well, I guess it's just you and me."

On the day of her release, a young white female nurse gave Dream the address and phone number of the local welfare office.

"They might be able to help you. If not, there's also the number of a shelter on the back. Dream, I wish you the best of luck. You haven't had one visitor since you delivered and I can see that's hurt you a great deal. I'm hoping things get better for you from this point on."

Dream seriously doubted that, but she smiled politely and thanked the woman for her concern. Things never seemed to work out for her no matter how hard she tried and the welfare system would be no different.

The older, stern looking caseworker looked over her wire-framed glasses, down at Dream.

"How old are you?"

"Sixteen."

"Hmp! Sixteen and a mother already," she said, shaking her head. "You young girls gon' learn. Most of ya'll seem to wanna learn the hard way."

Dream frowned and snickered at the rude woman.

Bitch, just gimme some fuckin' help! You don't know what the fuck I been through in my life. Walk a mile in my shoes and then talk this shit to me!

"So, am I eligible or what?"

"Well, since you're under the age of eighteen and don't have a secure place to live, the only thing we can do is send you to a either a group home or a shelter. They can help you find an apartment and start up yo' assistance."

"How long will that take?" Dream asked.

"Around thirty to ninety days."

"You want me and my baby to stay in a group home or a filthy shelter for three months? Why I just can't come pick up my check and food stamps every month?"

"Right now, it's the only choice you got. The State didn't tell you to go out and get yo'self pregnant now did it? You got no address, no plans and the State ain't gon' let you be out in the streets with no newborn baby. They'll take her from you first. So looks to me like you got a choice to make. I suggest you think about it and make the right one."

Dream resigned and agreed to take her baby to the shelter. Although rude as hell, the lady was right. Dream had nowhere else to go and she couldn't stand the thought of anyone taking her child from her. She was all she had in the world. It was her only choice besides taking her back to the house with Pieces.

She snatched the paper from the caseworker and collected her things. She walked out the Liddell Street exit and walked up to Grand Avenue to wait for the bus. Dream boarded the Olive bus towards downtown, to the Harbor House Shelter for Women and Children.

As she sat on the Bi-State transit looking out the window, a young girl with a toddler on one leg and a newborn infant in her arms, greeted her.

"Your baby is really cute. Is that a boy or a girl?"

"A girl," Dream responded.

"What's her name?"

"Destiny. I see you have two."

"Yeah, this is Mercedes on my lap and Porsche in my arms."

Two girls! I really feel sorry for you! Well, for them anyway. You better keep them away from men, especially the one's in yo' family.

"Is it hard?"

"Girl, naw. I take good care of my kids with my welfare check and I signed up for public housing yesterday so I can get me an apartment and not have to pay no rent."

"How much do you get on welfare?"

"Two-hundred and ninety-two."

Two-hundred and ninety-two dollars! Shit, I can make that in a few hours. If it wasn't for the way hoeing made me feel, I would put her up on game.

"That's all they give you? For two kids?"

"Yeah but I mean, its cool. I sell some of my food stamps every month to get my clothes, my hair and my nails done."

"Their daddy must be happy."

"Well, this one's daddy is in jail and this one's daddy is with his wife, so he don't want nothin' to do with her. But fuck it, I'm cool. I still get hollas like crazy."

As Dream watched them exit the bus, she thought of living on a monthly budget of three-hundred-dollars. She wasn't used to that and she knew she couldn't survive on it either.

She also sat back and thought of the repercussions she would face from Pieces once she went back to the house to gather her things and tell him she was getting out of the prostitution game. He would be upset, she knew that much, but to what extent she could only imagine.

Ebony had come home one evening and told Pieces she had met a man, fell in love and wanted to move in with him. Dream could still see the dried up bloodstains on the wall and the floor. He had beat Ebony something terrible.

"Nobody leaves me bitch! You hear me? Nobody!" he told her as landed his fist up against her jaw and forehead. His blows were both fierce and hard in force.

By the time Dream and Ebony left the ER at Barnes Hospital, Ebony's left arm was in a cast, two of her ribs were bruised and her face was battered and beaten.

Dream had never seen Ebony after that night. She had her new man pick up at the rear entrance of the hospital to avoid another run in with Pieces. But Ebony did leave Dream with these words:

"I'm sorry Dream, it was planned the moment he saw in you in the park. We set out to get you involved in making this money. I couldn't see past the money and the pretty things. I wasn't used to all that. But I am sorry, Dream, for getting you into this. You can do what you want, but I'm out. I found a real ma,n with real feelings for me and I'm out. You can come with me if you like, the choice is yours."

"So all that you told me in the park, was that all a lie too? About your uncles and your baby?"

"No, that part was true. It was used in the wrong way."

With that, Dream backed away and Ebony disappeared into the night. Dream often wondered where she was. Rumors flowed throughout the neighborhood and the stroll that Pieces had killed her. Little did the girls know, Pieces himself had started the rumors in order to keep the girls in check and to give them serious doubts about leaving him.

It had worked obviously, because as Dream exited the bus, walked across the street and waited on the Olive bus going the opposite direction, Pieces words towards Ebony burned in her ear:

"Let that bitch bleed and let that be a lesson to you! Nobody gets outta this unless I let 'em out! And the only way I'm a do that is when yo' pussy drops out from yo' body! And don't think you can run and hide, 'cause I'm just like bad credit, baby. I'll find you wherever you go!"

Dream walked towards the front door of the two family brick building and sighed. When she put the key in the lock,

Pieces was sitting on the couch, getting head from Brianna, his newest working girl.

He looked up at Dream and when he noticed the baby, he pushed the young girl's head to the side and stood up.

"Where the fuck you think you goin'?" he asked Dream, approaching her.

"To my room."

"Naw the hell you ain't! This here's a hoe house, this ain't no fuckin' daycare."

Dream sighed.

"So what am I supposed to do, Pieces? Where am I supposed to go?" Dream asked, looking down at her baby girl.

"Shit, why didn't you just leave the lil' muthafucka at the damn hospital? I'll put you up in a room at the Jefferson Arms downtown but it ain't comin' outta my cut. Now gon' in there and pack yo' shit. 'Cause baby or not, you still got tricks to turn and my money to make."

Dream struggled to be a full time mother and hoe at the same time. Most of the times, the stroll would have to come first. She would often have to leave the infant alone in the room while she went into the streets to handle her business.

Chapter Nine

The tears continued to flow down Dream's face as Pieces continued to heat the tip of his gun and insert it into Dream's now bloodied and blistered vagina. She tilted her head back and wondered what her next move would be. Pieces was obviously not going to allow Dream to walk away and strike out on her own. She'd brought in too much money for him. To him, she was a gold mine.

Yet through the agonizing pain, Dream assured her herself that if only she could make it through this torture Pieces was taking her through, she would do whatever it took to get away from him, set up shop in a different part of the city and be her own protection and pimp.

Once the pleasure he got from listening to Dream scream out in agony was gone, Pieces cut the rope from her arms, the ties from around her ankles and told her to get on her feet. She couldn't comply. Her body was hurting like hell and Dream just wanted to die right there on the spot. Pieces yanked Dream by the head and pulled her out the bed.

"Get up, bitch! No mo' free rides fo' you! You owe me two days of work, and I don't give a fuck if you gotta sell that muthafuckin' kid over there, you got three days to get me my money or the next time, bitch, it's yo' life!"

He gripped her by what was left of her blue T-shirt and slung her, causing her body to slam into the concrete door frame. She felt as if her bones had cracked from her skull down to her ankles. Dream hit the ground and tried to focus her eyes and see Pieces' next move through blurred vision. She seemingly saw it coming but her body ached way too much for her to avoid it. His foot came down across her ribcage both hard and intense. She winced, curled up in the fetal position and banged on the floor with her fist.

No more! I can't take no more! This is it for me, please! Just kill me. Don't beat me no more, please. I give up! I don't wanna do this no more! Please God, if your exist, let me die…

But those unspoken thoughts meant nothing to Pieces as he grabbed her by the hair and pulled her up to her knees. He swirled around the saliva inside his mouth until he built up a pretty good amount. He looked down at Dream's bloody face, smirked and hurled the wad of spit across her face.

"You ain't shit bitch! You wasn't shit when I found you, sittin' yo' broke down ass in the park. I bought you from the gutta, the gutta bitch, when nobody else wanted yo' ass, didn't care nothin' about yo' ass and didn't give a fuck if you lived or died. And this is how you repay me? You cheat me out my money? Bitch, I swear on my life, you lose any mo' of my money, I'll kill you and that bastard of yours, you hear me? Huh? Bitch, you hear me?"

With that, he slammed Dream to the floor and walked over to the door. He looked back at Dream and finalized his thoughts.

"Three muthafuckin' days Dream, or it's light out."

With that, he slammed the door. When he disappeared, Dream struggled to get back to her knees and crawled over to the bed so she could lift herself up. Her heart jumped as she heard the door open again. Dream just knew Pieces had decided to cut his losses and was coming back to kill her.

Who would really miss me anyway? My baby? Shit she's probably better off without me anyway.

Dream struggled to her feet but fell short and plopped down on the mattress just as the door opened in full view of the visitor.

"May I come in?" The woman asked Dream, peaking inside.

Kamry was a middle-aged black woman who often came by and checked in on the working girls of the Jefferson Arms, among other places. Kamry, known to the streets as Kam, stood at 5'9, 165 pounds and not only dominated but owned the streets when it came to whoring.

Born in the heights of prostitution, Kam walked the streets of St. Louis day and night, with hot spots in the Jeff Vanderlou Projects, Blue Myer Projects, LaClede Town Projects and the notorious Darst Webb projects.

Kam had serviced some of St. Louis' most elite social members, from the mayors, police captains, reverends and corporate execs, to the big time *balers*, out on the grind. Not to mention all the boyfriends and husbands she turned tricks with on the regular. Kam had the clientele to move mountains.

Butter brown skin, deep dark brown eyes and a lengthy hair weave often made Kam look like a model, but on the inside, Kam's body was like melted butter; it could spread any way you wanted it to. Her vagina was so rubbery and worn out from working the streets, she decided to leave the grime of the streets and open her own female escort service.

She didn't want the high class, saditty girls working for her. She liked the hustle and determination of the lower level street girls. She respected their desire for the grind and their ability to deal with whatever necessary for the paper chase.

For that, she went to the lowest of the low: The Ebony Motel, The Pink Slip Night Club, Lisa's Motel and the Jefferson Arms. Here she could find the pick of the litter. Most were young runaways or street girls running from their pimps and looking for a new way to do things. The one thing they all had in common was they all had problems and Kam always had the answers. It way her way to make sure that the girls she chose, were always indebted to her. She was sort of like Pieces, except Kam had the power to change lives in a way that Pieces couldn't. Most of these young girls were running from men or just plain tired of getting used up by men for pennies on the dollar.

By a woman offering them a new way, it meant more to the young girls, thus making them feel as if they could never repay Kam for her kindness in helping them out of their situations. For Kam, seeing Dream on the bed barely able to sit up straight from the pain, she knew she had yet, another perfect one.

"Oh, my goodness baby, are you alright? Who did this to you? Hold on. I'll get you some help."

"No!" Dream shouted. "Please don't... I know him, he's probably downstairs waiting to see if I'm gonna call the police or not. Don't do that, I'll be fine."

"Sweetie, you aren't gonna be fine if you don't get some help. He just beat the hell outta you. Look at you, you can't even see outta this eye. You can barely move."

"I'm good, trust me. I'm used to this. This ain't nothin'. Just go. I'll be aight."

"Until when? Until the next time he beats the fuck outta you or better yet decides to kill you?"

Dream tried to stand up to go and check on the baby but her legs didn't have the strength to cooperate. She leaned over, holding her ribs and wincing in pain.

"That's it, I'm calling the police."

It was part of Kam's plan to act *super* concerned. It made the girls even more loyal.

"Please!" Dream said through her tears. "I can't go. They'll take my baby from me if they find out what I do. They'll take her from me quick and she's all I got. I can't risk losin' her."

"No one's gonna take your baby from you," Kam told her, walking over to the dresser drawer and retrieving the baby. She took the baby to Dream and sat down beside her.

"Look, here's what we'll do. I can take you to the hospital myself, sit there with the baby until you see the doctor and if you need to stay, the baby can come home with me. I have a nice house out in Ferguson with plenty of rooms. I'll keep her with me until you get on yo' feet and can do better fo' yourself."

Dream pondered the thought for a minute. The last time she believed a person that offered to help her, she ended up in this position. She thought about the invitation but declined.

"Naw, but thanks anyway. I wouldn't feel right leaving my baby with someone I don't know. Like I said, she's all I got."

"No offense, but… what's your name?"

"Dream."

"I'm Kam. Well, no offense, Dream but do you know any of the people you lay in front of your baby and fuck fo' money? Now I'm just keepin' it real with you. You take a chance every time you lie down with a trick. He could go off and kill you both at any given moment. So what I don't understand is, if you gamble with yo' daughter's life like that, why not take a chance with someone who's trying to help you?"

Dream sighed within herself. In essence, what Kam had said to her made a lot of sense, but Dream still had reservations and as she would come to later find, there was a good reason for it.

However, at the time Dream could see no other options as she played back Piece's threat in her mind:

Three muthafuckin' days, Dream, or its lights out!

If nothing else, Dream truly believed in heart that Pieces would take her life without hesitation the next time. She had to escape.

Karen had made it perfectly clear that she wanted no parts of her daughter or her grandchild in her home. So, against her better judgment, Dream agreed to allow Kam to take her to the hospital and keep Destiny while she was under the doctor's care.

Maybe I won't even have to stay, she reasoned with herself.

Kam helped Dream to her feet, packed the baby a few sets of clothing and smiled to herself. She knew she had Dream right where she wanted her.

Desperation and co-dependence were the two greatest motivational factors in a street whore. Desperation brought forth the need to get money by any means necessary and co-dependence, whether drugs, alcohol, money or another human being, soon brought desperation.

Dream wasn't desperate enough for Kam just yet. Kam could feel that she was strong-willed, although Dream couldn't see it in herself and to Kam, that will needed to be broken. Kam also knew that Dream was a natural born hustler and survivor. Desperation broke the spirit of both and Kam needed to put Dream in a position where she could do nothing but bow down to whatever Kam threw her way. Unbeknown to Dream, Kam had been watching her for months.

She had plans for Dream and they didn't involve the tagging along of an infant. And as she called downstairs to her business partner, Big Ren and asked him for his assistance with Dream, Kam carefully began to put her plan in motion.

When Big Ren reached the hotel room and laid eyes on Dream, he knew that once again Kam had struck gold and picked a winner.

Dream kept her face down to the floor and refused to make eye contact with the two-hundred-forty-six pound bodyguard. She was too embarrassed at the way she looked and as she reflected back in her mind at the last time she went to the hospital at the hands of a man, Dream's soul became extremely sad.

She was tired; tired of fighting for the existence of her spirit. But she knew that this was the hand she was dealt and her only other alternative was to give up on life itself. Yet, inside the "belly of the beast" was where Dream drew her strength. And as she relaxed her aching body against the soft leather in the back seat of Big Ren's four door burgundy Chevy Blazer, she knew she had to continue to do whatever it took to maintain her existence out on the streets.

She knew Pieces would soon be looking for her and that meant she needed to get to some place safe, lay low for a few weeks and then get back out there and grind like never before. She had to find a place on the other side of the city for her and her daughter. Maybe even move across the bridge to East St. Louis. She'd heard that Brooklyn was poppin' when it came down to the street game.

When the Blazer pulled into the parking lot of St. Louis Regional Hospital on Delmar Blvd., Kam looked to her and smiled.

"Trust me, everything will be alright."

Dream had a gut feeling something was wrong. She just couldn't imagine at that moment what else could possibly go wrong in her life but soon, it did.

Chapter Ten

Dream could barely see the bright lights through her severely swollen eyes. Big Ren had carried her from the car into the ER, sat her down in a wheelchair and rolled her up to the admitting counter.

When the nurse saw the condition Dream was in, she immediately paged a doctor.

"Quick, help me get her in exam room one," the chunky black nurse screamed to a nearby orderly.

Dream was fading in and out of consciousness when the small framed, shorthaired Japanese doctor asked, "Do you know where you are, young lady."

Dream slowly shook her head.

"Do you know who did this to you?"

Dream rolled her head over to the side and pretended she had passed out. She didn't want to answer any of their questions. Karen's statement burning in her mind:

"You ain't finna have me all up in here with these white folks all in my business."

Dream couldn't let them find out what she did for a living. Couldn't let them know she was on the stroll because she couldn't stand to lose her baby to the system. She simply just wanted something for the pain, to get patched up so she could get back out in the lobby to be with her daughter.

"Ma'am, ma'am, can you hear me?"

Dream didn't answer but as the exam went on, she could no longer hide from the reality of the pain. When the doctor touched her side, Dream couldn't help but jump at the intensity the sharp pain sent through her mid-section. The doctor tried to calm her down and quickly instructed the nurse to start an IV so Dream could be administered Demerol for the pain.

"Ma'am, I need you to tell me what happened to you. Do you know who did this to you?"

Stop askin' me that shit! Do I know who did this? Hell yeah I know! A muthafucka I trusted. Fo' the second time in my life, I trusted a person that said they cared about me and ended up getting' dogged out. It's not the first time and it probably won't be the last. So quit fuckin' actin' like you so damn concerned. Nobody gives a fuck about me for real. Just hurry up and patch me up so I can get out of here before he comes lookin' for me. You can't protect me from him, he'll find me. Just…just like he found Ebony.

"No," she whispered. "I don't know."

The doctor looked to the nurse and shook his head. He knew Dream was lying to him but he couldn't make her tell him who had hurt her. An attack this bad could have only happened at the hands of someone who felt comfortable enough to spend some serious time, torturing her like that.

"Well," the doctor sighed. "We'll do the best we can to make you comfortable."

Once the nurse put the IV in Dream's arm and the first shot of pain medicine made its way through her veins, Dream felt groggy. She tried to fight it because she wanted to go out in the lobby and see if her daughter was okay. The constant fear of someone hurting Destiny played on her heart like a set of drums.

Yet, the medicine was too strong and soon it overtook her. Dream was asleep. By the time she had awakened, it was hours later and she was now in a private room, alone.

Her first thought when her eyes opened was of her baby girl. She threw the cover from her legs, tried to sit up and possibly swing her leg over the side of the side of the bed but she couldn't move. The medicine had her weak and slow in motion.

The nurse entered the room and walked over to Dream's bedside.

"My baby. I need to see my baby."

"Your mother took the baby home so you could rest. She said to tell you she'd be back in the morning."

"My mother?"

Dream's heart jumped with excitement at the thought of Karen coming to take her child home with her.

At least she's with someone I know, she thought to herself. *My Momma does still care. I knew in time, she'd come around.*

"Yes, that was your mother that came into the ER with you wasn't it?"

Dream's emotional high came crashing down as quickly as it rose. Kam had taken her baby home, not Karen.

"Oh, yeah."

The nurse took Dream's vital signs and propped up her pillow behind her.

"You should rest. I'll be back in a few hours."

"Ma'am, what time is it? I wanna call and check on my baby," Dream asked as she reached for the phone on the stand next to her bed.

"It's around twelve to one. The phones go off at twelve. They won't be back on 'til around six thirty. The television is off as well but you can get the radio on the TV. Maybe some music will help you to relax."

"Thanks."

Dream pulled the mobile TV over to her bed and began searching the stations for something to listen to. She would settle for anything to get her mind off where her child was. She rested the dial on Doc Winters and the *Quiet Storm* playing on Majic 108 FM.

As she lay there staring up at the ceiling, the song's lyrics took her by surprise. She thought back to the conversation she and Ebony had on her bed about music and how it always seemed to tell how you're feeling at the time.

"Everybody's got a story. Everybody goes through shit, just different shit," she remembered Ebony telling her.

"…I was born by the river, in a little tent, ohh and just like the river I been runnin,' every since. It's been a long time comin' but I know, a change gon' come, ohh yes it will. It's been too hard livin' but I'm afraid to die. Cause I don't know what's there, beyond the sky…"

Dream felt the tears flow uncontested down her cheeks. She simply couldn't imagine how her life had ended up this way.

What did I do as a child to make God hate me so much? Was wetting the bed really all that bad? I really wish he'd just tell me what I did to make Him this mad at me.

Dream cried a cry fit for the time of mourning. The truth was, in so many ways, she wished she'd die for real. The world had shown her nothing but agony for as long as she could remember and she honestly didn't see things getting better any time soon in the future. The melody had brought it out... all the tears she had buried deep inside her from the moment Ebony had told her, that only the strong survived out in the streets.

Dream rolled gingerly on her side and gripped the pillow for comfort. She allowed herself to cry out all her feelings. For in the morning was a new day. Only to Dream, the way her life was going, she silently prayed she wouldn't live to see it.

I don't wanna hurt no more…

Chapter Eleven

Dream struggled to walk and maintain her balance as she searched the lobby for Big Ren, Kam, and more importantly her baby girl. Her heart raced as she searched high and low for her baby. Just as she was about to head to the nurse's station and ask one of the nurse's to call the police so she could report her daughter missing, Kam rounded the corner with little Destiny in her arms.

"I had gotten so scared something happened to ya'll. I was about to lose my mind," Dream told her, reaching for her daughter.

"Dream, you know you not well enough to be tryin' to hold her. Come over here and sit down, then I'll give her to you."

Dream followed Kam over to the pastel flowered chairs in the waiting room on the third floor. Kam watched as Dream eased down in the chair beside her and held out her arms once again for her baby girl.

Kam listened attentively as Dream talked to her infant daughter. She was assured that Dream would do anything in the world to ensure the welfare and safety of her child. In Kam's eyes, she was just a step away from where she needed her to be. She had already begun not only whispering in her client's ears about a young beautiful girl, she soon would be adding to her team but she'd also began putting Plan B in motion just in case Dream didn't want to play ball.

Dream couldn't shake the feelings she had flowing inside her heart about Kam. For some reason, even though everything looked kosher on the outside, Dream felt something was wrong. She had dealt with the streets long enough to know when she was being played, but Dream couldn't figured out Kam's angle. She had seemed so genuine in her attempt to help her at the hotel and she was keeping an eye on her on her daughter while she recovered.

But why? Ebony always said that nothin' in life is free. People always have a motive for wanting to be in your life. It can be either a good one or a bad one, but everybody's got one. So I need to find out what hers is.

Dream sat her daughter on her right thigh and looked to Kam. "So, can I ask you a question?"

"You can ask me anything, Dream."

"Okay. Really, why are you helpin' me like this? I mean, what you really want from me?"

Kam shifted in her seat and smirked.

"I just wanna help, Dream, that's all. I mean, really help you. I'm not talkin' about no petty shit, either. I'm talkin' about really help you to stand on your own two feet. Control the stroll instead of the stroll controllin' you. There's an old sayin' among us older hoes and that is; Make that money, don't let that shit make you. Do you understand what that means, Dream?"

Before Dream could answer, Kam replied instead.

"No, you don't. 'Cause if you did, you wouldn't be in this situation right now. You would be in control of yo' own shit and capable of cuttin' out the motherfuckin' middleman.

Back when I was hoein', I had a pimp who used to beat my ass just like yours. But one evening, I had been out there on the streets fo' about three days straight and I was tired. My legs were tired, my jaw was tired and my pussy was tired. But up comes this nigga, tellin' me he wanted a down payment on a new Cadillac and that I needed to bring in mo' money that night.

Well, I told that muthafucka it wasn't happenin' and I couldn't go no further. He beat my ass so bad, broke my fuckin' left jawbone and two of my ribs. I had made a decision right then and there that it was time for me to be my own boss, run my own pussy and make my own muthafuckin' money.

We pay pimps for protection, Dream, that's it. So I got myself a bodyguard on my pay roll and the rest is history. I began to run the game and the game could no longer run me. Pimps ain't real 'hood niggas. They like to beat up on they hoes, to keep a sense of fear in 'em.

But ain't none 'em, got enough balls to go do a bid, 'cause then they'll be the hoes, you feel what I sayin'? Don't worry about his bitch ass, worry about that paper. Get on board with me and I'll teach you how to make it happen fo' yo'self. So, to answer yo' question, I'm helpin' you because you are who I used to be and I'm trying to help you get like me. It's as simple as that."

"So, there's nothin' in it fo' you?" Dream asked.

Kam giggled.

"But of course! This is business, baby girl. For me helping you, givin' you the game and shit, I too, will require a small percentage of yo' earnings. All I'm sayin' is that I'm gon' front you the clientele. You no longer gon' stand on the street corners waiting on a trick to pull up. I'm gon' allow you to stay at my house with my other girls and I'll hook you up with customers myself. And these ain't no raggedy ass niggas either. These are some of St. Louis' finest. Politicians, police chiefs, Reverends, the whole nine. So I'm talking money... major money. There's just one thing..."

Dream listened intently. The thought of making all that money sounded good to her, but she knew somehow there would be a catch. Yet Dream couldn't imagine the upcoming request Kam was about to ask of her.

"You can't be real to this game, not a true hoe in the game, with a kid on yo' hip. Is their anyone, anyone you know that'll take her in?"

"No, I tried that when I had her. I'm all she's got and she's all I got." Dream paused to gather herself. It truly hurt her to think of her and her daughter out here alone in the world.

"So you can't help me if I have to have my daughter with me?"

"You'll be limited, Dream. These niggas I fuck with are sometimes willing to pay a thousand dollars a pop, to spend one night with my girls. You can't make real muthafuckin' money with a baby, suckin' on yo' titty every two hours. And that's just keepin' it real."

Dream's heart felt heavy as she thought of her alternatives to accepting Kam's offer. She definitely didn't want to go back to Pieces' world, but she also didn't feel she was strong enough to go out there on her own.

But I can't give up my baby. I just can't!

Dream's eyes began to water and Kam sort of felt sorry for her. Dream wiped her eyes and kissed her daughter. She couldn't stand the thought of her life without her.

She glanced off down the hallway and her eyes fell on him. He was five-foot-seven, one hundred-sixty-five pounds, pure dark chocolate skin, with dark, soft eyebrows that connected slightly into a unibrow. His face was cleanly shaven with a perfectly lined hair cut and goatee. She had never seen a man look so good. Wearing a pair of navy blue slacks and a silk butter pecan colored shirt, he had a style so raw, Dream felt butterflies in her stomach just looking at him.

Her stomach did summersaults as he walked towards their direction and approached the nurse's station. Dream could smell his *Drakkar* cologne from where she was sitting and even though her inner thighs were severely swollen, her clit tingled as she inhaled his fragrance.

She watched as the nurse pointed in her direction and the handsome man turned to acknowledge when he saw her.

Dream immediately dropped her head and looked at the floor. She didn't want a man, especially a man that fine, to see her with a face all beat up and swollen.

But as the man came closer and called out her name, she was forced to face him, and finally she noticed the shiny metal badge on his hip and a huge nine-millimeter Glock on his side.

"Violent Crimes Division, huh?" Kam asked him, standing to extend her hand to him.

"Yes, ma'am. I'm Detective Williams; Garvonni Williams. I got a call concerning an assault against one, Dream James. And from the looks of it, I would assume it's you," he said, nodding towards Dream.

"Yeah, I'm Dream but I didn't call the police."

"The social worker here at the hospital did when you were brought in. Do you mind if I ask you a couple questions? Do you feel up to it or should I come back."

Dream looked to Kam. You could see the fear in her eyes. Pieces still had a hold on her and Dream couldn't imagine testifying against him in court. She couldn't risk her or her daughter's life like that.

"Maybe… maybe you should come back another time."

The detective studied her. He had seen her kind so many times before. But he had yet to see this level of fear in one of them. He could tell she had gone through a rough life outside of what she was presently going through. The fact that she couldn't even raise her head to look at him, by experience that told him that she had no self-esteem, no self worth.

Garvonni despised men who got their shit off on beating on women. They were cowards to him.

Put 'em in a cell with a real man and they'd bow down like bitches, guaranteed, he thought to himself.

He stretched out his hand to Dream.

"It'll only take a minute."

Dream sighed. She thought of Ebony and how she had disappeared. The reality was whether she went with Kam or not, if Pieces just so happened to run into her on the streets, Dream knew he would kill her.

She handed Kam the baby, stood to her feet and with the help of Detective Williams, went over to another private section of the ward to talk.

Chapter Twelve

Detective Williams helped Dream into her seat and offered to get her something to drink. Dream declined and never broke sight of the ground below her feet.

Garvonni took a seat beside her, making sure not to get too close. She was already afraid; he didn't want to come off to overpowering or overbearing as to chase her away before getting her help.

He really wanted to catch the man who did such a violent and horrible thing to what he could tell was really a beautiful young woman.

"Dream…uh, may I call you Dream?"

Dream shook her head. Although she refused to make eye contact with him, she could smell him. His fragrance was intoxicating to her. Her inner thigh muscles began to jump and her pearl tongue began to tingle. His presence was physically stimulating her, something she'd never felt towards a man before. Sex was just a job to her, plain and simple. Rarely, if ever, had she been attracted to someone of her own free will.

She closed her legs tighter, tried to focus and answered his question.

"Um-hum."

"Well, Dream, I know I'm a man and being in my presence may be very uncomfortable for you right now, and if it will be easier or if it will make you feel better, I can call a female officer to assist you. But believe it or not, I'm here to help."

Dream fiddled with her thumbs as the sound of his voice soothe her in a way she could've never imagined.

"This was a horrible thing that happened to you," he continued. "Who ever is responsible for causing you this kinda pain, with your help, I wanna make sure he pays for it."

"Why?" Dreamed questioned. "Nobody really gives a damn about what happens to me anyway. Girls like me, we get lost and be forgotten about out here in these streets and those who are supposed to care about you and love you, go on with their lives like... like you no longer exist. And if they don't care--the people God put here to care about you--why should anybody else give a damn, including you?"

Garvonni allowed his heart to empathize with her. She was trying so hard to put on this front like she was so tough but deep inside she was scared as hell and he knew it. The way she sat slumped over in the chair alone suggested that she seemed to have the weight of the world on her shoulders.

"Listen, Dream. There are people who really do care about what happened to you. I am one of those people. That's why I'm still here. I could've simply walked away the moment you said come back another time but I didn't. And that's because I wanna help. The reality is you could've very well been my mother or my sister. Men who hurt women, like this one hurt you, should not be allowed to walk the streets of this city... any city. I really do wanna help you, Dream, not just because it's my job but because I *do* care. But you've gotta let me help you. You've gotta trust me."

Trust you? Do you know how many times I heard that shit? The first nigga I trusted fucked me at nine years old. The second pimped me out. Never will there be a third! You can hang that shit up.

And why he gotta smell like that? Why he ain't come up in here with a regular uniform on? Why he gotta be dressed all "G" and shit? I'm feelin' shit I ain't never felt before. And he fine as hell! But I can't afford to trust nobody no more, fine or not. Naw, I'm good.

Dream slowly turned her head to face him and Garvonni had to swallow the lump that had unexpectedly built up in his throat.

"Your mom or your sister, huh?"

He looked to the ground and shook his head.

"My dad used to knock my mom around a lot when I was younger, up until the day he drank himself into the grave. My sister, who's only a couple of years older than you, thought that it was normal for a nigga to beat her 'cause that's all she came up around."

Dream was now looking at him eye to eye. Her right eye was swollen shut as if she'd gone twelve rounds with Roy Jones.

"Do you beat on women, Detective Williams?"

He held her one-eyed stare. "Never! Never have I raised my hand to a woman except to hug them. I've seen my mother cry too many nights and felt useless to help her because it was my dad who had hurt her. But now I'm a grown man and that's why I do what I do, for the mothers and the sisters, the daughters and well... for young women like you, who are afraid to imagine a future past this particular point in their lives. Women who are so gripped by the fear of these punks that you'd rather stay here in the comfort zone of pain because you're to afraid to be better or think you deserve better."

Dream's eyes began to water and Garvonni reached in his pocket and retrieved a handkerchief for her. He felt bad for making her cry but like all young girls in Dream's predicament, she needed to know that there was something good waiting for her on the other side of the humiliation and pain she felt at that moment.

"I apologize for making you cry or if I offended you in any way."

"No, you didn't. It's just hard sometimes to look back at my life. What it has been and what it is now. Things are what they are. I take this shit out here one day at a time. It's the only way I know how to survive. I never give much thought to my future 'cause I never expect to live through the night. I see girls die out here in these streets almost every day at the hands of some crazy ass trick or their overbearing pimp. Most of 'em lose their life over some nickel and dime shit. I don't know, I just figured my time would be comin' soon, too."

She leaned forward and looked around him to check on the baby.

"She's beautiful," he told Dream. "Maybe you should think of your future for her, if not for yourself."

Dream looked back. She understood what he what saying but in her eyes he failed to realize that life on the streets was about loyalty and survival by any means necessary. If your pimp found out you were crossing him or being disloyal to him in any way, that was automatically a death sentence.

Here he is talkin' about survival and a future, yet he's tryin' to push me to turn in Pieces. Yeah, maybe he'll get locked up fo' a minute but what happens when he hits the streets again? Who's gon' be there to protect me then? I do better off goin' with Kam. Maybe I can find shelter and safety with her for a while.

"Thanks anyway but I think I'd rather take my chances alone. Bringing that kinda heat to the streets or the stroll, is a sure way to get knocked at any minute. Like you said Detective, not for me but for my baby girl. I gotta survive the best way I know how and the way you talkin' ain't in my grasp right now. I appreciate you takin' out the time to talk to me and all, but I think I'll be okay."

Garvonni sighed and resigned to let Dream do things her own way. He had no choice. Sadly, he knew deep down inside that he'd see her again, next time possibly inside a body bag with an ID tag on her toe. He realized he couldn't force her to walk away from her life on the streets and he also knew that it was stone cold fear more than her will, that had her bound to the code of the hoe stroll.

Garvonni reached into the back pocket of his Dickeys and pulled out his brown leather wallet. From inside, he pulled out a business card and handed it to Dream.

He looked at the creature before him and he felt that same feeling he had felt with his mother all those years ago. He felt useless. He wanted to help her, but once again he had to accept the fact that he could not force her into anything. She had to want a change in her life. Until then, everything he said to her was falling on deaf ears.

"Call me if you change your mind."

Dream took the card and placed it in the pocket of her blue and white hospital gown. She looked down at his hand when she responded. She felt she couldn't really look him in the face after turning down his offer for help.

"Thank you for coming, Detective. I'll call you if I change my mind, but I really don't think I will."

Detective Williams patted her on the knee and smiled.

"It's okay. Just in case."

Her skin felt soft to him and he felt unexplainably emotional as he rose from the couch. His heart felt heavy as he extended his hand to her to help her stand.

When he walked her back to the waiting area where Kam and the baby were waiting, his grip was different and Dream noticed it right away.

His arms felt stronger and his hands more comforting and gentle. Garvonni too realized that he was holding Dream a little closer than before. Why, he didn't know. He just felt the need too.

Dream enjoyed the strength and the comfort she felt in his arms. For some unknown reason, she felt the one feeling she truly had never felt before, not since her father died. She felt safe. It was as if at that moment nothing or no one could hurt her. She felt a shield of protection coming from his touch, and in a moment of weakness, she allowed herself to lay her head against him as he guided her back towards the chair, next to Kam.

Garvonni felt warm when Dream rested her head on his torso.

Maybe it's what she really needs, a shoulder to lean on. He also felt a tinge of sorrow for her but he had to quickly get his feelings into check. *Don't get too attached to a case. This is the job, that's all. Damn! But she sure does feel good to the touch. It's a damn shame she's out here like this.*

When Dream noticed the look on Kam's face as they approached her, Dream quickly lifted up her head and acted as if was capable of walking on her own free will.

Garvonni noticed Dream's sudden defensive move and snickered at the expression on Kam's face.

The fuck is yo' problem?

Kam stood to hand Garvonni one of her business cards.

"For you."

Garvonni glanced at the title on the colorful card and smirked. "CEO, Ladies Unlimited." No questions were needed. He knew the company name all too well. Most of his violent crime complaints were associated with her escort service. Young girls and women alike, even some men, beaten at the hands of her musclemen for slow payment or shortage on a payment.

He handed the card back to Kam and chuckled.

"No thanks, ma'am. I don't deal with yo' kind. But I'm sure we'll meet again, real soon."

Kam sucked her teeth and smiled a halfhearted grin.

"That's what they all say in public, but behind closed doors, the story always change."

Garvonni looked back at Dream who was now seated and holding her daughter in her arms.

"Dream, you have my number." He looked to Kam and then back to her. "Take care of yourself."

As he headed towards the exit, he sighed to himself.

She can't know what she's getting herself into. That's the dirtiest bitch in the game.

Pulling out of the hospital parking lot, he added volume to the radio. The song blaring out over the speakers described the young breed of women he met on an everyday basis on the job, especially the one he'd just left behind.

"...Now Brenda's gotta make her own way. Can't go to her family, they won't let her stay. No money, no babysitter, she couldn't keep a job. She tried to sell crack but end up getting' robbed. So now what's next, there ain't nothin' left to sell, so she's sex as a way of leavin' hell. It's payin' the rent, so she really can't complain. Prostitute found slain and Brenda's her name, she got a baby..."

Garvonni brought the car to a stop at the intersection of Goodfellow and Delmar Blvd. He sat there at the light and bit down on the inside of his lip.

It wasn't the fact that Dream had refused to tell him who had assaulted her, that he was used to. It was the other level of the game he knew she was about to experience at the hands of Kam and company.

But even a 'hood grown, streetwise Detective like Garvonni, couldn't imagine Kam's next move.

Chapter Thirteen

Dream spent the next four days in the hospital without a word from Kam. The number she had given Dream was to an answering service and Dream had quickly grown tired of leaving countless messages.

She was to be discharged in an hour and she couldn't find anyone to come and pick her up. Her ribs were still wrapped up and her face, still a little black and blue but the swelling had gone down in her eye.

The only clothes she had were the heavily blood stained clothes Kam had brought her to the hospital in, so the nurse had given her a pair of sky blue surgical scrubs to wear home.

Dream's eyes began to water as she thought of the last time she had worn a hospital outfit out of the front door of a hospital. She wiped her eyes and tried to shake off the feelings the memories had brought back to mind.

Some shit never changes for me. Maybe it's just the way things are supposed to be for me.

As she sat on the bed swinging her legs, awaiting her discharge instructions, paperwork and prescriptions, Kam rounded the corner and entered the room.

"You ready to go?"

Dream turned to find Kam, standing there, perky yet empty-handed. Dream's smile faded as quickly as it came. She slid off the bed, walked past Kam and peeked around her into the hallway looking for her daughter.

"Where's my baby? Where's Destiny?"

Kam held her hand up in the air.

"She's fine. I'll tell you about it when we get in the car. Now hurry, we have things to do."

"Is she in the car? Who is she in the car with? Don't tell me you left her in the car with Ren!"

Dream charged around Kam and grabbed what little things she had off the bed and began to hightail it out of the room towards the elevator despite the tenderness in her wounds.

Kam snatched Dream by the arm, which caused a sharp pain to shoot through her ribs.

"Don't make a scene," she whispered. "I said, we'll discuss it in the car."

Dream saw the iciest look in Kam's eyes that told her not to mumble another word. Then within a split second, she smiled the warmest, motherly smile at Dream.

What just happened here?

The nurse brought in a wheelchair for Dream and gave her all her discharge papers.

"Now I have appointments set up for you all day today. We begin at the hair salon," Kam told Dream as she sat down in the wheelchair and they headed for the elevator.

"Then, it's the nail shop and the mall. I've got company comin' over to the house tonight. And don't worry, I've got the perfect makeup to hide that eye."

Big Ren helped Dream into the back seat of the black Blazer and then helped Kam on the other side.

When the car door closed and started on it's way out the parking lot, Dream turned to Kam.

"Okay, we're in the car now. Can I finally ask where my baby is?"

"Well, once again she's fine. The way I see is you needed a lil' time to yo'self. A lil' time to get things where you need them to be in yo' life. I told you back at the hospital that you can't be a hoe, not a real hoe, with a baby bouncin' on yo' hip. You said you had no where to take her so I took the liberty of finding a nice, safe place for the little one until you rest up and rise up. The longer you had to worry about another mouth to feed, the longer you was gon' be at the bottom of the game."

"A safe place? And where is that? 'Cause that's the way we need to be goin'. I need to see my baby."

Kam just shook off Dream's statement and nonchalantly replied, "Later."

Dream's heart began to race and a sense of fear gripped her so strongly she thought she'd loose her breath. Her eyes began to water, her voice continued to elevate, and without thinking, she reached over and grabbed Kam by the breast of her three hundred dollar Gucci shirt.

"What did you do with my baby? I want my baby! Where the fuck, is my baby!"

Dream was hysterical at the thought of someone having her child. It was hard enough to deal with Kam's having her while she was in the hospital. Now some stranger had her and Dream wanted to know who.

Her eyes expanded at Kam's reaction to her grabbing her in her chest. Kam reached across and slapped Dream hard across her cheek, which forced Dream to release her shirt and grip her jaw.

"Don't ever put yo' fuckin' hands on me again or I swear to God, Dream, I'll kill you! Do you hear me? Ever! It's nothin' fo' me to have Ren pull this muthafucka over and throw yo' ass out on the corner some damn where, you understand? Do you?

Now sit yo' ass back and shut up. You wanna get gangsta on me? Let me break it down to you. According to my calculations, you owe me roughly around twelve grand fo' this lil' hospital stay of yours, since I signed the paperwork the night you came in. Two, fo' the room and board for yo' kid and at least five grand fo' handlin' yo' business with Pieces."

Pieces? What business?

"So now, that's almost twenty grand alone. Now if you can come off that, I can take you right over to where she's stayin', you can pick her up and we can part ways, no harm done. But, if you can't, and I'm so sure you can't, then you might as well lay back go along to get along 'cause you won't lay eyes on her until all my money due to me, is paid!"

What?

"No…no…you can't do that!" Dream pleaded with tears rolling down her face. "Please, you said you were tryin' to help me. Why are you keeping my baby from me? She's all I got in the world, you know that! Please! Please let me see my baby!" she pleaded but to no avail.

Kam continued let her pleas roll right off her shoulders. In her eyes, Dream was refusing to see the big picture. She was really doing her a favor. Kam felt as if she was freeing Dream to make as much money as she needed to get on her feet, and Kam enough money to continue to be a ruler in the game.

Dream resigned to the back seat and stared blankly out of the window.

Maybe I should've gon' with Detective Williams. Maybe I can still call him and tell him I'm in trouble when I get to the shop. But what can I say? I don't even know where she took her, and if I say somethin' to get her in trouble, she'll never tell me.

Just suck it up for now, Dream. Play this game the right way today and maybe by the end of the day, she'll see I'm willing to play the game her way and she'll take me to see her. Then I'll call Detective Williams in the mornin' and tell him what happened.

But the emotional pain was too intense for Dream. She lay her head against the head rest and silently let the tears roll.

Kam pulled out her cell phone and made a call back to the house, informing the girls that she'd be in later and to send all her calls to the answering service and to make sure all the arrangements were together for later on that evening. She had great plans for Dream's introduction to her clientele.

She hung up the phone and glanced over at Dream and smirked. She finally had reached the level Kam needed her to be at in order to achieve her goal. All she had to do was string her along by believing she would see her baby again if she played her cards right, when in reality, Kam had already sold the baby girl on the black market to an adoption agency over across the river in East St. Louis, Illinois. Kam told them that the mother was killed in a horrible car crash while the baby was in her care, and the mother had no family she could take the baby to. Kam wanted her to have a good home.

Being that the adoption agency was under the rug, they asked no questions and raised no suspicions. Without any remorse or any regret, Kam sealed the deal with the agency for fifteen grand and never looked back.

Dream was comatose as she stared out the window, thinking how empty Kam had just made her life.

The blazer came to a rest in front of the *Jitter Big's* Hair Salon on Grand and Natural Bridge Blvd. Kam came around to the passenger side door.

"The sooner you snap out of it Dream and accept it, the sooner you grind, get money and go get her," Kam lied.

Dream stepped out of the truck and wiped her face. She had to accept the hand dealt to her, at least for now.

Kam gave her a pair of shades to cover her eyes and pointed towards the shop. "Now, are you ready? Let's go get this money."

Dream took the shades from Kam and placed them across her face. She sighed and held her tongue. She had to play ball and do it Kam's way.

She followed Kam inside the shop, put on a half ass smile as Kam introduced her, sat down in the chair and began on a journey she had no idea, was on a winding road to hell.

Chapter Fourteen

Garvonni couldn't shake the thoughts he had of Dream in his head. He had seen cases like hers before but for some reason, she was different. He didn't know why, she just was.

Maybe it was because she reminded him of a girl he once knew. A girl he had a chance to save, but didn't. He could hear her screaming in the distance behind the Tangy Recreational Center, right near the Sumner High School he was attending as a junior…

Practice had ended a little late for the young up and coming Bulldog starting defensive safety. Garvonni had just moved to the north side of the city after spending the majority of his life in the Berkeley area. The county life had only semi-prepared him for the life on the notorious north side, but thanks to his grandmother who lived on the corner of Evans and West Belle, Garvonni got his street lessons taught to him the hard way.

Coming up in the Blood and Crip era, Garvonni joined the 49 Crips for protection. It was necessary at the time because gang bangin' was high in the 'hood, and if you didn't belong, you were an outsider, bound for bloodshed.

The Crips were runnin' rampant at the time and things were out of control in the city. Shootouts, drive-by's and murder was the name of the game. Garvonni got along to get along, meaning, he too had blood on his hands. But no matter what, he had morals to the game as well… no kids, no old folks and no women. He had a mother and a sister of his own. He would protect them with his life and he knew other niggas felt the same.

But Crip love was bound by more than loyalty, it was bound by life. To walk away was an early death sentence and it was made known to Garvonni by the murder of his best friend, right in front of his eyes.

Mango and Garvonni played ball together and dreamed of one day sharing the same field opposite each other in the NFL some day. The night was set, the plan was laid down and the targets were marked. The only problem was, the payback was scheduled the same night as the high school playoff game. Garvonni chose to miss the game, saying he had a death in the family. If only he had known, death was certainly around the corner.

Mango, on the other hand, had foolishly decided to go to the game and the after party with his girlfriend. When the bloodshed was done, the major playa's in the gang went on the hunt for all those who had not shown up and disobeyed the order to lock, load and ride.

In a crowd full of high school party goers, the gang walked in the auditorium, spotted Mango and unloaded their Glocks, hitting him at least seven times throughout his body.

Garvonni had attended the party once the deed was done, partly to have fun and partly for an alibi. When he saw the head honcho enter the gym, he searched the room vigorously for his friend. But by the time, he spotted him, the shots had already rang out and his best friend had fallen to the floor.

Garvonni rushed through the crowd of frightened people, pushing his way against the flow and kneeled down at his dying friend's side. There was nothing that could be done as his life had slipped away within a matter of seconds.

Garvonni took the message to heart and at that moment, clearly understood that he could never go against the grain, not unless he was prepared to die.

As he walked home from practice, he crossed the side lawn of the Rec center. Her screams were magnified as if someone had placed a microphone to her lips. Garvonni followed the screams with all intentions of helping whoever it was that was in trouble but as he rounded the corner to the back far, east side of the Rec center, he stopped dead in his tracks.

Her face was bleeding profusely, her clothes dismantled and torn. Her damn near, lifeless body lay with her legs spread apart, underneath one on his fellow gang bangers.

When one of the boys saw him approaching he drew his gun, cocked it and aimed it right at Garvonni's head. But once they made eye contact and saw that he was one of their own, he dropped his gun and stretched out his hand for Garvonni to meet up and shake his hand, Crip style.

But Garvonni couldn't move. His eyes were focused on the creature below his feet on the ground. Her battered face looked familiar to him. Her name was Keisha and she sat right beside him in English class. She was a beautiful girl. She had a great personality and was always friendly to him. Now, here she was, damn near lifeless beneath his feet.

"You want some of this shit, man?" the high-yellow gang banger asked, humping in and out of the now unrespondent young girl.

Garvonni's sister's face flashed before his eyes. His heart went out to the young girl but he knew if he tried to interfere with what was going down, he'd be lying there right beside her.

His life and his dream of playing pro football flashed before his eyes and Garvonni selfishly chose his dreams over saving her life, a decision that would come back to haunt him the rest of his life.

"Naw, naw, dog. I'm good on that shit."

He turned to walk away from his friends. The one with the gun, Sammy Gee, called out to him.

"Aey, Aey Gee man, don't let me hear about this on the block, you feel me?" he said, aiming his gun at Garvonni and moving his lips in a popping motion.

Garvonni understood exactly what he was hinting at and when he heard the gun shot upon reaching the corner, he ran as fast as he could to his grandmother's house, went straight to his room and cried.

The bangin' life had cost him so much; his best friend, a rap sheet and now the life of a innocent girl he had hoped to someday, become good friends with.

As he sat there on his squeaky twin-sized bed, Garvonni decided he had to find a way out of the gang. He had to find a way to exist with them in the 'hood but not be apart of the things they did. He had vowed his loyalty to them when they jumped him into the crew and he knew they wouldn't allow him to walk away with his life.

With tears rolling down his face, as the ten o'clock news flashed the yellow tape around the Rec center, he vowed to come up with a plan.

As the months went by, Garvonni catered to the leaders by pulling off the small jobs in exchange for being allowed to invest time in his NFL dream.

"So, what you wanna go to college fo', nigga?" Garren, one of the major playas on the Crips, asked Garvonni before sending him on a pick up run for three kilos of cocaine.

"College ain't fo' no nigga's in the 'hood. That shit is fo' them preppy niggas and them white boys."

"Yeah, but if I don't go, I can't play ball, and you know I'm tryin' to get to the pros, man. And I can make it, I know I can. I mean, I ain't braggin' or nothin' but I'm pretty raw."

Garren inhaled his blunt and pondered what Garvonni had told him. Garren felt he was the one of the more lenient ones on the boss squad and he always like the way Garvonni kept his mouth shut and showed a lot of heart whenever he was asked to get down and dirty.

"Yeah nigga, you are pretty raw with that ball shit. I'll holla at the other bosses and I'll make somethin' happen... on one condition."

Garvonni sighed. He knew there had to be a catch but it didn't matter. Whatever he had to do to get away from the game, he'd do.

"I don't give a fuck where you go or what the fuck you do in life when you make it big, nigga and you come back to the 'hood and shit, pushing Limo's and shit. Holla at yo' boy. That's my only requirement. G?"

"It's "G", man. I got you."

They shook a C'd up handshake and Garvonni went on to pick up Garren's dope on his ten speed bike. But when he arrived, he was greeted by two masked men with guns drawn at his temple. It was a jack move, a carefully planned jack move.

Garvonni didn't know what hit him. The first blow came from the left side with a nine millimeter. It led a series of blows to his head and body, ending with a gun shot wound to his knee, blowing his knee to shreds and insuring an end to his football career.

He would later learn that it was his fellow gang members sent by Garren that robbed him and made the point clear: You never leave the game, not without consequences.

Over the next several years, the game had faded and most, if not all the boss squad, were either dead or doing life in prison. Garvonni joined the Police Academy and was now Detective Williams.

His past had haunted many nights. Waking up in deep sweats, he often saw the images of the people lost in the struggle, mainly Keisha and Mango. Keisha's images bothered him the most. She favored Dream in his eyes and to him it was the main reason he felt compelled to try to save her.

He made a U-turn at the light and sped his way back to the hospital. He was determined to make her talk, determined to help her and determined to finally put his ghosts to rest…

Chapter Fifteen

The days turned to weeks and the weeks turned to months as Dream turned into the hoe of the century. Kam and the game had turned her out in the deepest sense of the word. She was now into doing anything and everything to pay Kam back the money she owed, in hopes of laying eyes on her baby girl again someday soon.

Kam kept her going with promises of visiting the little girl each week but when it came time to deliver, there was always a last minute client that Kam said needed to be served. Dream, now one of Kam's most poplar hoes, was now trickin' with men and women alike.

Kam worked Dream a constant twenty out of twenty-four hours a day, with minimum rest in between her tricks. Dream was being literally dragged through the gutter and the fact that she'd picked up a lil' habit along the way didn't help matters much. She had begun taking "uppers" to stay awake and make all the money she could.

In Dream's eyes there was no time to sleep if she ever wanted to hold her daughter again. But the uppers took a toll on her, and soon she needed "downers" to bring herself back down. Things were looking bad for Dream, and before she knew it, she was hooked. She often self-medicated herself to avoid the pain of losing her little girl and to deal with the countless tricks she provided erotic company to on a daily basis.

She had gone from just a simple prostitute to an all out around-the-way-girl. Meaning, she now offered the services of every part of her body to get paid. All the glory and the hype of the game Kam used to trap her came crashing down into a harsh reality for Dream.

There were no extravagant clients, no mayors, no police chiefs and no big time ballas or businessmen. It was the constant traffic of the same riffraff that Dream had dealt with on the streets. Kam just disguised it better.

Dream still faced forcible entry into areas of her body she cared not to sell. She still faced a stiff hand or two from some over-aggressive tricks and above all, she still lost her money from time to time due to being robbed. But she hung in the game because she knew it was the only way to one day be able to see her daughter again.

The night was January the seventh, Destiny's birthday and Dream felt the raw emotion of missing her child even more.

I wonder what she's doing. I wonder if they even know it's her birthday. She's walking now, I know. How could she take my baby from me like this? How? She lied to me. Everybody lies to me. They only tell me what I wanna hear to make me do what ever the fuck it is they want me to do. And my stupid ass falls for it every time. I should've listened to Ebony. Everybody had ulterior motives, nothin' in life is free. Everybody's help comes with a price.

Dream began to cry.

Maybe she's better off without me anyway. My life ain't nothin', I ain't nothin' and from the looks of shit, I ain't gon' never be nothin'. My momma was right. I was born to be shit. And maybe they takin' real good care of her and she probably don't need me no more. But why can't they see that I need her? She's been the only thing I feel like I did right in my life. The only good memories I have since Daddy died. And now they've taken that from me too. I'm tired. I'm so fuckin' tired!

Dream wiped her face and reached over to the nightstand for her downers. The small brown bottle of pills was half-full. She had made up in her mind that she simply wanted to end it. She felt she had nothing to live for if she couldn't have her baby back. She wanted to just go to sleep and never wake up.

She picked up the bottle of downers and read the warning on the label; *Do not take more than the prescribed dosage.* She unscrewed the bottle top and poured twelve of the tiny powder-blue pills into the palm of her hand. She reached down on the floor next to the bed and grabbed the bottle of *Wild Irish Rose* she was drinking and began dumping the pills into her mouth, chasing it with the cheap wine.

She sat there on the bed thinking back over her life, how she had gotten to this particular moment in time. In her heart, Dream knew she was a good person and she simply couldn't understand why all those tragic events had come her way.

Looking back, she honestly questioned herself: What had she accomplished besides the mastery of being a good hoe? She hadn't received an education past the ninth grade. She hadn't ever heard her mother, or anyone for that matter, ever tell her they loved her except Ernest and he single handedly had begun this road in her life.

She had lost the only man she loved; her father. She had lost the only woman who understood her; her Nana. She had used her body until the walls of her vagina hung low like horse nuts, and the once radiant skin on her face now showed forceful signs of premature aging.

The only thing beautiful and good to come out of her life was Destiny and now she too was gone. Dream felt she had nothing left to live for, nothing else to hope for and nothing left to give.

The mattress on her queen-sized bed began to sink in to her. She felt her body began to float, her arms and her legs becoming heavier by the second, her vision beginning to blur and her breathing becoming labored and her heart rate decreasing. She didn't fight it. In fact, she gave into it. She was prepared for it, she was ready for it... she wanted it.

Wanted it all to go away. Didn't want to feel any more pain, heartache, have bad dreams... and no more shame.

The tears rolled down her face as she lay her head back against the pillow and closed her eyes. She began to feel the peace of her soul over take her. Before she went out, she whispered one last thing: *"I love you Destiny! I pray you never know the kind of mother you had... a hoe!*

With that, the room became dark... so terribly dark.

Chapter Sixteen

The call came in over the radio on his side:

"…Code 1 (acknowledge this call), *be advised we have reports of a female reported to have overdosed at 4116 Enright Ave. Code* 3 (proceed with lights and sirens). *Request a car on the scene. Emergency Response is already in route, 10-14."*

Garvonni reached for his radio. "Ten-four, I'm in the area. I can head that way."

"Ten-4, Detective Williams. Ten-5 all units. Be advised Detective Williams is 10-76 (enroute) *and will be securing the scene. Also be advised that the address is known on the hot sheet for 10-82* (probable prostitution), *so take all bio hazard precautions."*

Garvonni hit the sirens and the lights on his dark bronze Chevy Lumina and made a left on Union Blvd. He lit up a Kool cigarette. He always had to light up before he went to a crime scene. He never knew what to expect and as he rounded the corner onto Enright and noticed all the mayhem in progress, he was glad he did.

The Sixth District patrol units had all the escorts and all their paying customers lined up against the black gated fence. When Garvonni spotted Kam, he immediately began search the line up for a familiar face… Dream.

When he didn't recognize any of the girls, his stomach tied up in knots. He threw the Lumina in park, jumped out of the driver's side door and ran for the entrance to the gate. As he passed Kam, they made eye contact and her facial expression told Garvonni that his instincts were right. Something had gone wrong with Dream.

He ran up the front steps to the stained-glass front door, flashed his badge to the officer guarding the entrance and blew past him in search of the EMT's.

He rounded the corner in the hallway and headed up the black spiral steps to the second floor. When he reached the far back part of the hallway, the EMT's were exiting the room with a body on the gurney. The young white male EMT was straddling the body while performing CPR on the victim.

"Come on! You're much too young to go like this. Breathe, dammit, breathe!"

As the gurney passed him, Garvonni flashed his badge once again and held his hand into the air for them to stop and let him see who the victim was. When he looked down at the young girl, he wanted to cry. There was Dream, eyes closed, mouth wide open with foam running down the side of her cheek. Her hair was a mess and she was naked from the neck down.

"Can you save her?"

"We're tryin', sir but we need to go, now!"

Garvonni backed away and shook his head. He called out to the men rushing the gurney down the hallway, "And hurry up and put a sheet on her. Show her some respect."

James Cain, Garvonni's longtime friend and part-time partner, walked up to him with a puzzled look on his face. He knew Garvonni seldom allowed cases to get to him. But the look on Garvonni's face said otherwise. His expression was worth a thousand words.

"Hey man, you aight?"

Garvonni exhaled a deep sigh.

"You know her?"

Garvonni hesitated, then shook his head.

"Sorta. You remember the call we got up at Barnes Hospital on the day of you and Lena's anniversary and I told you to go ahead, I'd handle it alone?"

James looked confused.

"Remember, the one I told you the pimp had beat senseless and then the vic hooked up with ol' girl, the madam?"

"That's her?" James asked in disbelief.

"Yeah man, that's her. I was so pissed off that day when I went back to the hospital looking for her. I missed her by about an hour the day she checked out. And I turned around to go back the day I had originally took the complaint to tell her that fucking with that bitch wasn't the best way for her to go. But I got a 187 and I had to re-route. Now look at her."

"Yeah but didn't you tell me that she didn't want to turn the nigga in who beat her ass?"

"Yeah but still, I felt like I was starting to get through to her a little in the hospital waiting area and maybe--"

James cut him off mid-sentence.

"Come on, GW, you been in this shit long enough to know that you can't save anybody who don't wanna be saved."

I couldn't save someone who wanted to be, he thought to himself.

"Once these girls get out here and let some punk or wanna be gangsta turn 'em out, there's not a whole lot we can do about it except eventually tag 'em and bag 'em."

Garvonni didn't like what James was saying but in his heart he knew James was right. Most of the girls he ran across were okay being treated the way their pimps treated them and no matter how hard you tried to keep them off the streets, they always found their way back.

But he felt something different with Dream. He knew that somewhere deep inside she wanted a better life. She was just too scared to make the first step. Even her actions that night told him she was tired of the way she was living.

He wanted to help her--he needed to help her. He had demons in his past that he needed to make reparations for. The life he could've or should've saved had haunted him every night. He couldn't live with two on his conscious.

"You can handle this, right?" he asked James, searching his pockets for his keys before realizing he'd left them inside the vehicle.

"Yeah, I got it. Go."

"I'm gonna follow them to the ER," Garvonni said, taking off back down the flight of steps.

He ran out of the front door and headed for his truck. As he passed the gate, once again he made eye contact with Kam. He stopped dead in his tracks and walked over to her. He closed in on her and stared her in the eyes.

"You wanna tell me what happened here?"

"She OD'd. What else is there to tell you?"

Garvonni's eyes narrowed and his jaw tightened.

"Look, Detective. Dream is a grown woman. She ain't no baby. I ain't got time to be holdin' nobody's hand, twenty-four hours a day. She chose this life, it didn't choose her."

Garvonni leaned into Kam's ear and whispered to her, "You sick sadistic bitch! If she don't come out of this, I swear on my life, I'm gon' make you pay!"

"Are you threatenin' me, Detective?"

"Oh no, I'm not threatenin' you. I'm makin' you a promise. I will personally see that you are thrown up under the jail if that girl don't make it through this."

With that he walked away but then turned and doubled back.

"Doesn't she have a baby? Where's her kid?"

Kam looked down at the ground.

"I don't know. She says it's stayin' with her mother or some shit like that."

Garvonni snickered and told Kam she would see him again real soon. On that she could bet her life.

"I'll be lookin' forward to it," Kam smirked.

"Country bitch!" he muttered to himself as he climbed into the front seat of his Lumina, closed the door, made a U-turn and headed down Enright to Delmar, Delmar to Kingshighway and to Barnes Hospital once again.

"Fuck!" he shouted as he pounded his fist on the dashboard.

"Let her make it. *Just let her make it!"*

Chapter Seventeen

When Dream was forced to open her eyes by a gagging reflex, the first thing she saw was a big plastic tube that had been shoved down her throat. A middle-aged light-skinned female doctor was standing over her, upper end of the tube in hand, pouring a black substance down the tube. It was a charcoal mixture to absorb the pills from inside her stomach before they could filter out to the rest of her system and poison her to death.

Dream gagged for her breath but the tube felt as if her throat had swollen shut around it.

"Ms. James, I need you to fight that feeling and lay back. I need to get this down to your stomach as soon as possible. I'll try my best to move as fast as I can. I know this feels uncomfortable to you."

Dream searched her mind and tried to remember exactly how she'd ended up here in the ER getting her stomach pumped. She vaguely remembered the pills, taking a few and chasing them with wine.

Then she remembered the reason she wanted to die: Her baby's first birthday. She felt the pain all over again. She sobbed silently because of the tube in her throat. The tears flowed down her cheeks freely, Dream just closed her eyes and cursed God for saving her life:

Why won't you let me die? Are you just keeping me here to punish me some more? You let all this happen to me and now when the pain is to much for me to carry any more, I try to end it and you won't let me. Why do you hate me so much?

Dream just stared up at the ceiling as the lab technician pricked her with the needle and drew her blood.

Her eyes drifted off to a familiar face coming through the door.

What is he doing here?

Her heart raced as he came closer to her bedside. The doctor instructed him he would have to wait outside in the lobby area until they had stabilized her and then she could talk to him.

Dream made eye contact with Garvonni and with that tube down her throat and that look in her eyes, Garvonni saw Keisha's eyes staring back at him.

Dream turned away quickly.

I bet he thinks I'm one crazy ass bitch. But like everyone else, he just don't know.

Garvonni relented to the doctor and proceeded to exit the room.

Finally, the bottle with the charcoal mixture was empty and the doctor proceeded to remove the tube from Dream's throat. "This is gonna be a little uncomfortable, Ms. James but bear with me, okay?"

Dream nodded her head and tightly squeezed her eyes together as the pump came up her esophagus with difficulty and force. It felt as if her entire stomach lining came out with it, but in essence, she was throwing up black charcoal everywhere, her stomach involuntarily giving up everything inside of her. Her eyes watered as she hurled, scrunched over the side of the steel bed rail.

Make it stop! Please, make it stop!

It seemed as if it took an eternity for her stomach to settle down. Although as the handsome familiar figure came through the door, she wished she could hurl some more, that way she wouldn't have to face him.

He eased in the room after softly knocking on the door.

"So, we meet again. How you feelin'?"

Dream looked off to the wall.

"Can't you look at me and answer that one for yo'self?" she whispered.

"I'd rather hear it from you."

"I'm sure you know what happened already or you wouldn't be standin' here right now."

Garvonni thought back to Kam's words as he stood in front of her at the metal gate: *"I guess the lil' junkie couldn't handle her shit and fucked herself off."*

"I got yo' so called employer's version but I'm here to get yo' version. I'd like to hear yo' version."

"What does it matter? Last time I saw you, I was here! Now I see you again and where I'm at? Back in the same fuckin' place. That sentence alone should tell you that I fucked up. Once again, I made some dumb ass choices and paid for it three times what I owed."

"Then let me help you this time, 'cause if I recall correctly, I tried to at our last meeting but you decided against it with your employer's help. Now here you are, three seconds from death because of that same fuckin' employer and it's still up to you, Dream. It's still yo' call. I can't help you if you won't let me. If you continue to choose to protect the people that hurt you in this way, there's nothing I nor anybody else will be able to do to help you."

Dream stared off at the ceiling.

Maybe he's right. Maybe I could tell him everything. Kam, Pieces, her baby girl...everything. Maybe he really can find her.

"So you really here to help me or you got somethin' up yo' sleeve too? What, you get some kinda reward or somethin' for bringing people in? Is that yo' real aim? 'Cause if that ain't it, why don't you just put the shit on the table. I'm so tired of people disguising their real motives behind fake ass concern for me.

I wish muthafuckas were real enough to just come out and say shit like, 'Aey, Dream, check it. I think yo' ass is fat, yo' lips is pretty and I heard you get down for the grind. I want you to get out there and sell some pussy fo' me. Make me rich while I give you crumbs fo' using up yo' body like a roll of tissue, everybody wipin' they ass with you'."

Garvonni looked at her. He really felt sorry for her. He knew that the only way to help, was to gain her trust. She wasn't gonna talk to anyone she didn't trust and with good reason. She was done trusting the words of others. He understood.

He told her, "I feel you on that one, but you have to understand that most of the people you deal with in your, um, profession, are cold hearted muthafuckas that don't give a damn about anybody but themselves. Their goal is to make you fear them, owe them and do anything to please them, for whatever reason or whatever hold they have over you.

Niggas that call themselves pimps are straight pussies. Most of them wouldn't last three minutes in the penitentiary. They like to dominate and control women because deep inside they have that same feeling of inadequacy and no confidence in themselves to get out there and become somethin'. So instead, they try to turn that fear against those who are more fragile than themselves.

Do you really think most of these piss poor ass pimps got the balls to get out on the block and grind like these *real* nigga's grind? Rob, steal and deal to make it happen fo' themselves and they families? Naw! They ain't built like that. That's why they need young, naive and broken young girls such as yo' self. They gotta catch you when you're young because unless she's really down and out or strung out, he can't get that shit off, not on no grown ass woman."

Garvonni walked over to Dream's bedside and stared down at her. She felt uncomfortable with him being that close to her. Her body began jumping again at the smell of his cologne. She turned her head and looked away from him.

He continued, "The glamour in the beginning is attractive, I understand that. But at this moment, right now, you should be able to see that all it does is take from you. Your youth, your vitality, your femininity, your morals and yo' soul. Tonight, you almost lost yo' soul. And the one thing you need to ask yo' self, is this: Is it worth it? I mean *really* worth it?"

Garvonni took out his wallet from his back pocket of his , dark blue Polo jeans and once again handed Dream one of his business cards.

"Call me after you've thought about it."

Dream took the card from Garvonni and looked at it for a moment.

What he's sayin' does make sense, but shit, I thought the same damn thing about Pieces and Kam. They always come with that bullshit to reach out to yo' problems but they only offer fucked up solutions.

Dream watched Detective Williams open the door to her room and she called after him.

"Detective Williams, no. It's never been worth it but I just thought it was the way shit was supposed to be for me. I want help, really I do but it's so much shit in my life, I wouldn't know where to start."

"How about the beginning?" Garvonni said as the doctor walked passed him, into the room as he held open the door.

"Um, sir, I need you to step outside for a minute, please. I need to discuss something private with Ms. James," the doctor said.

Garvonni nodded as he looked to Dream.

"I'll be right outside." *Damn, perfect fuckin' timin'! I finally get her to start talkin' and here comes her lil', Minnie Pearl lookin' ass.*

He walked over to a seat in the waiting area and called James on his cell phone.

"What happened with ol' girl?"

"Shit, some minor shit. We couldn't hold her though. You know how Cap's ass is. I tried to get him to bend a lil' bit, but he was just like Novocaine."

"Novocaine?"

"Yeah, he just wasn't feelin' me."

Garvonni chuckled. His partner was always clowning and cracking jokes. Garvonni didn't mind because it kept him up during some hard days on the job. Plus he knew that no matter how much he clowned, when it came time to get down, he got down, 'hood style.

They had been partners for over six years since graduating the Academy together. They had both made the grade of detective at the same time.

"What up with the girl?" James asked.

"Stomach pump. Seems to be okay. Fucked up in the head behind a lot of shit. But finally comin' around. She was about to tell me some dirt on our madam but the doctor came in to talk to her. So I'm gonna hang out here until the doc's finished and then I'm gonna see if she's still in the mood fo' talkin'."

"Well aight then. I'm about to take my ass home and see if my wife's off the rag yet. Accordin' to her, she been on three weeks now, but I think she just don't wanna come off that ass."

"Aey, man, that was definitely T-M-I. I keep tellin' you, I know we partna's, but there is some shit I don't wanna know."

"Aight, man, holla if you need me."

"You got it," Garvonni said and hung up the phone just as the doctor was coming out of the room.

He stood up, put his phone back in the clip and headed for her door. But before he could push it open, his radio went off, a code 42 (aggravated rape) had been reported.

He had to go. He was the lead detective on duty.

He peeked into Dreams room and her back was turned to him. He figured she was asleep and so he told himself he'd be back in the morning but unknown to Garvonni, Dream had no plans of being there we he got there.

Chapter Eighteen

Dream balled up into the fetal position and cried until she couldn't cry any more. She had had enough. What else could go wrong, what else must she endure in her lifetime without being allowed to go over the edge?

The doctor's words burned in her mind and in her heart: *AIDS?*

"I'm sorry, Ms. James. Apparently you've had sexual relations with someone who was infected. And just one time is all it takes. HIV can lie dormant in your body for a long time and may take up to ten years to show up on blood tests."

"I know this is difficult for you, Ms. James, especially on top of everything else you've been through tonight. Is there anyone here with you?"

Dream's heart felt the weight of the world rest down upon it. "No," she whispered through her tears.

"Anyone you'd like for me to call and let them know you're here?"

Dream almost chuckled at that question. There was no way anybody was gonna have anything to do with her now that she had AIDS. Her family didn't care about her in the beginning, they really wouldn't fuck with her now, and Dream knew it.

"No."

"Well, a social worker will be in with you shortly to talk to you about not only what we just discussed, but also about your overdose tonight, okay? She's going to ask you a serious of difficult questions and we're going to need you to be honest."

"Questions, like what?"

"Well, you're a health risk to the community, especially in the line of work I'm told you do. You could have spread this to a great deal of people. We have to know the names of every person you've slept with since you've been sexually active."

Dream look at her like she was as stupid as that sentence that came out of her mouth.

Bitch, I'm a hoe! I done fucked hundreds of men in my life and some women too. Do you think I know they fuckin' names? Do you think they actually want to sit and hold conversation with me? Introduce themselves to me and invite me over they fuckin' house? How the fuck am I gon' know they names?

Dream's blood began to boil and she gripped the pillow in her arms so tight, that if it were a person, they'd be dead. Her memory reconstructed the day Ernest took her virginity, stole her youth. It reflected on the day Pieces introduced her to a world far too advanced for a young teenage girl, but perfect for vultures such as himself. She remembered the way Kam promised to help her but ripped the one thing away from her she could call her own.

It was as if you removed her heart from inside her body and placed it down inside a cooler full of ice. Her heart grew colder and colder the more they crossed her mind.

They had taken everything precious and special about being a young woman from her and now she had been served a death sentence--one that was sure to make her suffer in the process.

She had been feeling kind of achy lately but she would never have imagined this. Dream had always thought from what she'd heard from the other working girls, that AIDS was a gay man's disease. Now she had to face the harsh reality that it was now her tragedy. That it would soon take her life as well, for she'd heard, there was no cure.

But Dream had other plans. She wouldn't be the only one who suffered. She wouldn't be the only one whose life would be limited. She wouldn't be the only one who'd die.

She looked at the doctor and said, "Sure, but can you send her in about twenty minutes? I just need some time alone first. Take in everything we just discussed."

The doctor patted her on the thigh and told that was fine, then she left Dream alone to be with her thoughts, a move that allowed Dream more time to burn inside with fury and hate for each and every person that had destroyed her life.

She recreated the familiar scene of taking out her IV from her wrist, grabbing her clothes from the chair and putting them on. She got to the door and forgot the detective was supposed to be waiting outside for her.

Shit, what if he sees me?

She hopped back into the bed, pulled the tube to the IV underneath the cover with her, and hit the button for the nurse to come to the room.

"Can I help you?" the young preppy white voice came over the speaker.

"Um, I'm looking for the detective that came here to talk to me. Is he still out there in the lobby?"

"I'm sorry, ma'am but I saw him leave about fifteen minutes ago. Is there something else I can do for you tonight?"

"No thank you, that was I needed to know."

Dream flipped the cover from the bed, sneaked over to the door and peeked out.

Damn, this shit is so déjà vu*!*

When the coast was clear, Dream headed for the stairwell and walked through the lobby, out to Kingshighway Blvd.

She didn't know what her next move or even her first move be, but she did know this: These muthafuckas was about to pay for what they had done to her!

Chapter Nineteen

Dream wandered deep in thought and aimlessly towards the north side of the city. In her purse, she had a little over three-hundred and forty-seven dollars. The Bi-State bus was nowhere in sight so Dream decided to keep walking until it arrived.

Her first mission was to cop a piece, something very small, concealable, yet very powerful. She wanted something she could handle. She hadn't put her plans together yet, nor had she thought far enough ahead to an anticipated ending. All she knew at that moment was that she wanted something badly. She wanted *revenge.*

Revenge for all the things they had done to her over the years to ruin her life. Revenge for the way they had all manipulated her mind and emotions. Revenge for all they had taken from her… her mind, her body and her soul.

Dream boarded the northbound bus at West Pine and Kingshighway Blvd. She rode until the bus stopped at the corner of Lillian and Kingshighway where she connected to the 41 Lee bus. Dream pulled on the rope to indicate she wanted to exit at Lillian and Thrush.

When the back doors opened, she climbed down the steps and crossed the street, walking east, past all the half vacant houses until she reached the one she was looking for.

Dream had never come to the dope house alone before. Most of the time she tagged along with Pieces when he came to pick up his product or he needed something for protection.

She was nervous as hell as she walked up the crooked concrete steps onto the front porch. Her hand shook as she knocked gingerly on the door. Her stomach quivered with butterflies as the rough and raspy voice came blaring through the wooden door.

"Yeah?"

"Umm, I'm lookin' for someone named Cali. I don't know him personally but could you tell him someone gave me his name? Umm, I'm lookin' fo' some help."

The door cracked open with the chain still attached and Dream couldn't see anything more than a fraction of his face. She looked down towards the doorknob and saw the light from the outside street lamp bounce its reflection off of a shiny dark object.

"Who gave you my name?" the man asked.

Dream cleared her throat and spoke softly.

"Pieces."

"What you want? You lookin' fo' a stone or somethin'? Some of that boy, what? If so, you need to go to the side door."

"No, I...I don't need anything like that. I need to buy somethin' else from you."

Cali took a good look at Dream and studied her face and body.

"Don't I know you? Ain't you one of Pieces ol' hoes?"

Dream flipped off the remark. This was no time to be defensive. He had something she needed.

"Yeah. So anyways, I need to buy a gun. A small handgun that I can carry in my purse... for protection."

He raised his eyebrow.

"It's getting rough out here. These new up and comin' hoes don't respect the game no more."

He nodded his head and asked, "How much you got?"

"About three-hundred."

"I think I got somethin' you can get down with."

He unlatched the door and let Dream inside. The smell almost made her throw up. It smelled like dog shit and dirty laundry, mixed with sewage.

Inside the living room, the grey furniture was old, ragged and heavily stained from only God knows what. The floor was checkered black and white, with tiles missing in almost every other square. The walls were lined with spray painted words and gang signs. She was standing in the living room of a hoodlum, who rep'd the 36 Bloods to the fullest. She didn't give a fuck. All she wanted was what she came for; the missing piece she needed to put her plan in motion.

As she paced about the front room, she glanced into the hallway towards the back of the house. What she saw simply amazed her. Coming down from the ceiling was a big L-shaped pipe that ended down near a hole in the floor. Beside it was a built-in water faucet that flowed continuously down into the basement.

Dream had heard the girls on the stroll talk about how the ballas they tricked with often had a similar layout inside their dope houses. It was the quickest was to get rid of dope if the police kicked in the door. No more waiting for the toilet to refill and flush. The constant flow of water under pressure sent the dope right down into the sewage line, making it virtually impossible for the police to find anything.

"So, what you think about this?" he asked her as he walked back into the living room holding a black, .22 automatic pistol with a silver and pearl handle.

Dream took the pistol in her hands. She had never held one before but the touch of the steel against the palm of her hand sent chills down her spine. She rubbed her hand across the top of the gun and smirked to herself.

Ain't no muthafucka gon' ever hurt me again. Not with my new best friend at my side.

"So you want it or what?" Cali asked.

"Yeah, I want it. How much is it gon' hit me for?"

Cali cocked his head to the side and sucked his teeth. He looked Dream up and down. Dream rolled her eyes, knowing where his thoughts were at that moment. "I mean..." he started in, walking closer to her. "I'm sure we can work somethin' out. Maybe a bargain as to where, you won't have to come off nothin'. You look like you real nice underneath that skirt, and I'm sayin,' maybe we can make each other happy."

Happy? Muthafucka I got AIDS! How the fuck is fuckin' you gon' make me happy? Niggas kill me with that shit. Why do they think sex fix everything? The shit's been fuckin' me around my whole life.

She responded, "Umm, naw. I just wanna pay you and gon' about my business. You know how Pieces is about his money."

"Yeah, I feel you on that. But check this out. I just called Pieces on the phone in the back room, and uh, he said that you owe him a lot more bread than what you tryin' to spend with me."

Cali could see the fear in Dream's eyes when he mentioned Pieces, knowing she was at his house. It was as if she'd seen a ghost. He seized the opportunity to try his luck.

"Yeah, he also said fo' me to keep you here until he got here and he'd make it worth my while. So as I see it, it would beneficial to you to play a lil' ball with me. I mean I can tell him that when I came back from the back room you was gone already. That is, if you wanna play ball."

Fuck, why muthafuckas always tryin to leverage yo' pussy against you, like it's God or somethin'? It's just pussy, damn! Mine ain't no different than these other hoes but I swear, muthafuckas act like they gon' die without it.

Then Dream thought back to her present medical condition. She almost chuckled. Instead, she reasoned with herself.

Hmm, ain't that some shit? I'm already holding a nigga's death sentence in my hands. These muthafuckas wanna keep tryin' to use me? Well, I'm a leave 'em with somethin' they'll never forget nor get rid of; startin' with this muthafucka right here.

Dream looked to Cali and smirked.

"So what you talkin' 'bout?"

"You know what it is, ma. I wanna a shot of that. All of it."

Dream's bottom lip curled up in disgust. He was just like all the others. It was time…time to lay it down.

Cali walked over behind Dream and gripped her breasts. His touch felt just as disgusting as the others. She inhaled a deep breath and blew out her frustration at the world. Only this time, she took solace in knowing that she wouldn't be leaving that night empty-handed. She would get what she came for and leave with the satisfaction of knowing that she was about to come out on top.

"Aight," Dream said, nodding her head and pointing towards the back room.

"Let's do this."

Cali smirked and led Dream down the dingy hallway to the back bedroom. It was just as, if not more disgusting, than the living room.

Damn, it's funky as fuck up in here.

The bed was piled with dirty laundry and lined with filthy sheets. The clothes poured off the bed down onto the floor. Smelly shoes were thrown about, along with dirty dishes filled with mildewed food, spread across the dressers.

Cali wasted no time undressing, removing his wholly tank top, and his belly flopped immediately over his dirt-ridden gray shorts. Dream almost puked at the site of all the beaded up hair on his chest and stomach.

Great, a fuckin' werewolf.

She simply stood still in the doorway, staring in disbelief as he continued to undress. He pulled off his pants, only to reveal an immature sized jimmy stuffed tightly between two outrageously huge thighs that were stuck together.

No wonder he gotta pay fo' pussy. This muthafucka is gross!

To Dream though, the crusher came when he took off his Nike's. The smell almost caused her to pass out, as the aroma of sour mop filled the air.

"What you waitin' fo'?"

Second thoughts began to run through Dream's mind as she clutched the .22 inside her palm.

"Should I call Pieces and tell him to come on through? I got somethin' fo' him?"

Dream was furious at that remark but she held her tongue and began undressing. She pulled off her shirt, followed by her bra, skirt and panties. She walked over to the bed and sneered at the thought of lying down on top of all the filth.

Cali began throwing clothes down onto the floor and plopped down at the top of the bed. Dream could've sworn, she saw a cloud of dust rise up and fill the air.

She eased down on the bottom corner of the bed, followed by Cali. She grimaced as his hands reached out and touched her once again, his fingers, blistered and rough.

"Damn yo' titties soft."

Damn yo' shit feel like concrete.

"Come on up here and let me sample some of that mouth."

Dream couldn't imagine wrapping her lips around his shriveled up jimmy, but decided to just go ahead and get it over with. It wasn't like all her tricks were the cleanest of people. She had mastered the art of holding her breath and then exhaling so as not to inhale the smell of toxic balls.

His jimmy was so small it kept falling out her mouth. In her head, she chuckled. She continued to attempt to blow him off until he asked her to bend over.

But Dream had other plans. She wanted him to taste her, fill his mouth with every germ, every diseased molecule her juices could provide.

She stood up above him and stroked his matted hair.

"Don't you wanna taste me?"

"Shit, I didn't know that was part of the package. How I know you clean?"

No, he didn't!

"Shit baby, Pieces keep us at the clinic. You know his motto. 'A broke hoe, might as well be a dead hoe.' He ain't gon' keep us around if we can't make him no money and you gotta be clean to do that."

She gripped the back of his head and guided his lips to her breasts. His lips were dry and cracked. It felt like he was rubbing a pumice stone against her nipples.

"Let me lay down," she said. She squirmed across the bed and put her hands underneath her head so her hair wouldn't touch the mattress.

Cali got down on his knees in front of her and began teasing her inner thighs with his tongue. Dream knew the role to play. She squirmed and tensed up her body like he was driving her crazy just, at his touch.

Cali spread her lips apart and started his journey to taste the forbidden fruit, not knowing, he was about to taste the kiss of death.

Dream wanted to cum, she needed to cum in order for him to get the full outcome of her plan. She closed her eyes and began to imagine. A man, a dark man. So sexy and suave. His walk, his talk and oooh, his smell. She remembered him. Remembered everything about him that day. The darkness of his eyebrows, the intoxication of his cologne. The roughness of his voice, still vocalizing the 'hood in him.

Detective Williams played upon her mentality like African drums beating in the wilderness. She felt him, she wanted him…she craved him. The thought of him made her spine tingle and her "mommy" respond with a gush of juices flowing freely into the mouth of her user. She smiled as she released. She felt the power of changing his life, and she liked the way it felt. She loved it!

Cali thought he had laid it down, but little did he know that credit went to a man she had dreamed about on several occasions whenever she needed to take her mind into a fantasy world of passion and play. He was her fantasy and she used him often to escape her world.

As her juices flowed she moaned, "Get it baby, get it all!" She was back to reality and talking Cali into gobbling up her pain and her pleasure.

The she felt a rush that she couldn't explain. The thought of him living a life of torture in the near future had her excited. And at that moment, she wanted more. She wanted more people to suffer--those who had made her suffer over the years. She wanted them to live with the pain she had lived with all her life. Wanted them to feel what she felt.

Her mind tapered off to the radio and the lyrics that flowed from the speakers. The words spoke her feelings and she smiled an inner smile that for some strange reason, soothed her heart.

"…Well there's no more, sleepless nights, no more heartache and no more fights. See now all that has changed. I found somethin' to ease my pain. And it don't hurt now, no not now…"

At that moment, Dream tasted the bittersweet flavor of an inner place within her mind. She tasted *revenge.*

Chapter Twenty

The night came and went as Garvonni stepped out of the shower to begin his day. He was glad to be awake. He didn't sleep very well. The dreams he was experiencing had him tripping.

The first thing on his agenda was to go to the hospital and talk to Dream.

I gotta get to her before she changes her mind about helping me and herself.

He dressed in a pair of navy blue Khaki pants, a white, long sleeved T-shirt and a dark brown pair of loafers. He put on his gold watch, his diamond stud earring and his diamond chipped gold necklace, with it's matching cross. He brushed up his waves and put on his favorite Polo cologne. He clipped on his radio, his department issued side arm and his cell phone to his waist.

He grabbed his car keys and headed for the front door, only to be halted by the sound of the house phone ringing. He backtracked to the kitchen and picked up the receiver to check the number on the Caller ID. It was his baby sister, Unique calling to tell him the news of someone he once ran with, getting shot the night before.

"Sammy? You sure it was him?" he asked her, stunned.

"Yeah, I just saw it on the Channel 5 morning news. He got popped on the west side over by Maple last night. They say he was tryin' to rob some nigga and the nigga upped on him and killed him."

"Damn!"

"Wasn't ya'll like super tight back in the day?"

Garvonni exhaled.

"Yeah, you can say that, back in the day."

He hung up the phone and shook his head. He was the last one of the four to still be alive. The last of the crew left to face his destiny for what happened to Keisha that faithful night.

Garvonni had often wondered how his part would play out, having to one day answer for not helping the young girl.

The others had already paid with their lives and his heart raced at the thought of his demise. He often told himself that doing the work he did made up for the all the wrong he did back when he ran with the 49 Crips.

But now, he wasn't so sure. He felt as if his time too would soon come to a head. So Garvonni decided that he might as well make the best of it and help as many people as he could… starting with Dream.

He got into his Lumina and headed up for the hospital. Along the way, he thought of the frail woman he had left there night before. There was something else going on with him where she was concerned, but he just couldn't afford to find out what it was. This had to be all about the job; at least that was what he kept telling himself. But deep inside, Garvonni knew that it was also about redemption--redemption of the past, redemption for all his mistakes, redemption for his soul. He *needed* to help Dream more than he *wanted* to help her.

He hit Goodfellow Boulevard and headed South to Page Ave. As he rounded the corner, he did a double take. He could have sworn he had just seen Dream boarding the Page bus going towards downtown.

That can't be her! There's no way they would've let her out of the hospital this soon. Not in the shape she was in last night, he reasoned with himself.

He shook off that thought and assumed it had to have been just a young girl who favored Dream. He continued down Page Blvd., until he made a right on Kingshighway. He turned up the music on the radio, trying to clear his mind before he had to face her again. He didn't know what he would say to her, he just knew it was now, down to crunch time. It was now or never.

If he allowed her to be released from the hospital and not be able to elicit her help or get her to accept his help, he knew she would find her way back to the streets. He went over it a million times in his mind, the points he wanted to stress to her, the things he felt he needed to get through to her, but as he drew closer to Barnes-Jewish Hospital, nothing he could think of to say made any sense to him.

He cleared his thoughts and humbled his mind to the music playing over the speakers. The words were not only making sense to him, they moved him.

"... as the sun sets and the night goes around, I can feel my emotions comin' down. But now, as time goes by, I cover up my face, sayin' to myself, tonight I'll forget. Tears, tears, fallin' down like the rain. Tears, tears, another heart knows my pain..."

As he pulled up into the Emergency Room parking lot, Garvonni exited his car and headed for the sliding doors. When he entered the hospital, he walked through the main lobby to the West Pavilion and boarded the elevator to the fifth floor.

He walked up to the nurse's station and approached the thick framed, black female nurse. He flashed his detective's badge and commanded her attention.

"How you doing, ma'am? I'm here to speak with Dream James. I got a call last night and had to leave. Is it alright to speak with her now?"

The nurse looked to him and nodded towards the small Asian doctor walking towards the station. "I think you ought to speak with the doctor, Detective."

"Aight, thanks."

Garvonni approached the doctor and once again flashed his badge.

"I was just wondering if it would be okay to speak with one of your patients; Ms. James?"

The doctor looked down at her note pad and suggested that Detective Williams follow her to the waiting area.

Garvonni didn't like the feeling he began to feel down in his stomach. Usually when a doctor asked you to come to the waiting area, it was bad news. *God I hope she didn't die!* he silently prayed.

When they reached the lobby, the doctor pointed him to an empty seat, took the seat beside him and said, "I'm afraid speaking with Ms. James won't be possible."

Garvonni's stomach tied up in knots.

"Ms. James left the hospital last night."

"You released her in the shape she was in?" he asked in disbelief.

The doctor held up her hand.

"No, we didn't release her. The attending physician went in to consult with her about some things and told her that a social worker would be in to talk to her. By the time the Advocacy Worker got to the room, she was gone. She left without notifying anyone or checking out. We have no home number or address for her."

"Damn!" he mumbled. He had missed his chance. By now, Garvonni figured, she was back on the streets and back to business as usual.

"I will tell you this, without breaking privacy issues, we need to find her so we can get her some help... serious help."

Garvonni felt the same way. He had to find her. He had to pull her away from Kam and all the hell she had been going through. But Dream's overdose incident had given the police enough reason to temporarily shut down the escort service, so Garvonni had no idea where Kam would have moved her operation to.

He looked to the doctor.

"Aight, thank you for your help, doctor. I'll do my best to find her."

As Garvonni rose to exit the waiting area, he reached for his radio. "Central, this is Detective Williams."

"Ten-4 (message received). Go ahead, Detective."

"I need an APB (all points bulletin) put out for a black female. Name: Dream James. DOB: 7/25/1972. Hair: black. Eyes: brown. Height: 5'5, approximately 140 pounds. No LKA (last known address). Wanted for..." he paused. He had to think of a good reason for bringing her in besides his own personal goals. "Wanted for witnessing a 187."

"Copy that. All cars on duty, 10-5 (relay). An APB has been issued on a black female..."

As the dispatcher put out the description of Dream to the rest of the local force, Garvonni's mind flashed back to the young girl he saw boarding the bus on Page Avenue. *So it was her! Dammit it!*

He placed his radio back in its holster and walked towards the door.

The doctor called after him, "Detective, we really need you to get her back here as soon as possible."

Garvonni nodded his head at the doctor and headed for the elevators.

He hopped back in his car and with accelerated speed and headed down Kingshighway, back to Page Blvd. He figured he'd follow the *Page* bus route and see if she was hanging out on any of the corners, trying to pick up some work.

He rode all the way to Jefferson Ave. before he yielded to the fact that he'd lost her again. He decided he would circle around the area, until a call came in from his partner, James.

"Damn man, you been incognito since last night. What you been layin' up in?" James asked jokingly.

"Shit, man, I'm tryin' to get some help on bringin' down the madam. But my only source disappeared from the hospital last night, unnoticed."

"The OD?"

"Yeah, her. And I'm ridin' around tryin' to see if I can locate her. I rode right by her ass earlier, gettin' on the fuckin' Page bus but I didn't think it was her, cause of the condition she was in last night. But check this. I think if I can find out where the madam is doin' her side hustle at, I can put my finger on her."

"Shit, did you try the Ebony?"

"Ebony Hotel?" Garvonni asked.

"Yeah, you said you seen her gettin' on the Page, right?"

"Yeah."

"Well, that's right on the bus line and you know Ebony's is famous for trickin' and shit."

Garvonni chuckled.

"You right, man. Damn why didn't I think of that shit? J-Man, where would a nigga be without you?"

"Shit, nigga, that's easy. Probably headed the same place as Bobby and that bitch Whitney's marriage."

"And where the fuck is that?"

"Nowhere!"

They laughed.

"Nigga, you a fool," Garvonni said.

"Hold on man. This is Cap."

Garvonni made a U-turn and headed for the Ebony hotel, only to be redirected by James when he clicked back onto the line and said, "Head to Lisa's man. We got a 187. From what Cap just said, some nigga got popped with his dick in his hand."

"Aight, six minutes."

Garvonni hung up the phone and sneered.

Damn, what the fuck! I gotta find this girl, and every time I try to get a hold of her, something fuckin' happens!

But what Garvonni didn't know was he would arrive within minutes of Dream at the hotel...leaving that is, once again.

Chapter Twenty-One

When Dream boarded the Page bus, she was still riding high on the adrenaline she felt from the night before. The power it had given her to have sex with a nigga, knowing she was carrying a death sentence.

Maybe that's it. Maybe I should get back out on the stroll and leave all these muthafuckas with a lil' somethin'. All these nasty muthafuckas who prey on young helpless girls like me. These fuckin' perverts who get off shovin' they dicks down bitches' mouths and treatin' them like they ain't shit.

She was deep in thought, planning a revolution of male genocide, when she saw a familiar face boarding the bus. She hadn't seen it in years, but she'd know that face anywhere. She could never forget its features. His hair had slightly grayed, his weight had picked up about thirty pounds, and he now wore glasses but she still knew, without a doubt in her mind, that it was him.

Dream looked around at all the seats on the bus. The only one available was right next to her. Unexpectedly, she felt no butterflies, no fear nor the option of moving. She actually wanted him to come and sit next to her.

The man took the seat beside her, opened his newspaper and began reading. It instantly pissed her off that he hadn't recognized her.

How can a muthafucka forget a girl he molested over and over again? How can he not know the face of a nine-year-old girl he was fuckin' 'til she was fifteen?

The more she thought about it, the angrier she got. She thought about just getting off the bus but she refused. She refused to let him off the hook that easy. She refused to let him off the hook, period! She would *make* him recognize her if necessary.

"Excuse me sir, do you have change fo' a dollar? I need to get a transfer."

The man reached down inside his pocket and pulled a handful of change. He placed four quarters in her hand and put the rest back inside his pants.

"Thanks."

He looked right into Dream's face and yet he still didn't know her from a can of paint. That infuriated her.

"Ernest? Ernest is that you? I didn't even recognize you," she lied.

"I know you?"

She wanted to spit in his face right then and there.

Fuck you mean, do you know me? You bust my pussy open at nine fuckin' years old, muthafucka. How the fuck you don't know me?

Dream just bit down on the inside of her jaw and smiled a half ass smile.

"It's me, Dream."

Ernest eyes bucked open as if he'd seen a ghost.

"Dream? Little Dream?"

She nodded her head.

"Hey, baby girl. I've been wonderin' where you been. I ask yo' momma all the time have she seen or heard from you."

He just stared at her.

"My Little Dream. You know I used to love me some Dream. Look at ya! All grown up now, filled out all nice and healthy."

You could see the spit in his mouth drooling down the side of his chin.

"I hear you a workin' girl, now."

Dream twisted her lips.

"A workin' girl? Who told you that?"

"Oh, I hear's thangs. Is it true?"

"Depends. Can you pay to play?"

"Oh, I can pay! Matter of fact, I just cashed my check. How much you gon' charge me to get some of that all-grown-up-now pussy?"

Dream wanted so bad to stab him in each of his beady eyes that were undressing her on the bus. But she had other plans.

"I'm sure we can work out a discount, fo' old times sake."

She rang the bell to stop the bus at Grand Ave. Then, she and Ernest boarded the Grand Ave. bus to Lisa's Motel. She told Ernest to pay for the room and to use his ID because she didn't want any trace left on paper that she had been there.

When they entered the room, Ernest's hands felt as if they multiplied. He started grabbing Dream all over, rubbing his hands across her breasts and her ass.

"Oh yeah, baby, I missed this!"

His touch felt overly-gross to Dream, and she felt like gagging. But the opportunity was too great for her to pass by. The chance to leave the man who destroyed her childhood a death sentence, a long and suffering death sentence, outweighed the disgust she felt for him at that moment.

"So, how's my momma, Ernest?"

"She aight, I guess. I left her alone shortly after she put you outta the house," he said, pecking Dream on the back of her neck with his dry and crusty lips.

"I couldn't be with her no more after that. Hell, the only reason I stayed with her so long was to get to you. My lil' sweet pussy. After she took that away from me, there was no reason fo' me to stay around."

Dream actually had to chuckle at that one. She had mixed emotions about what Ernest had just said. On one hand, she was glad to see him leave Karen because of the way Karen had chosen him over her own blood. But on the other hand, it made her want to kill him more because he'd not only used her, but he'd used her mother, too.

"I still see her from time to time though, and I always asked her 'bout you."

Dream was curious to know Karen's response.

"And what do she say?"

"That you's a lil' hoe now. Always have been. But that don't bother me to hear her say that 'cause hell, befo' you was anybody's hoe, you was mine, ain't that right, baby?"

This muthafucka is crazy fo' real! So I was yo' hoe? Well, that's cool; let me show you what a hoe I can really be.

"Ump."

"Yeah, I used to love me some Dream. Pussy was tight, pure and untouched. Taught you how I liked my dick to be sucked and all that. You got pretty damn good at it too. Yeah, but I bet it's even better now, ain't it?" he said, pushing his jimmy into the back of Dream's ass cheeks.

Dream's stomach turned. She hated him, pure and simple. The man that she once thought was the only person who really loved her besides her daddy and her Nana, finally expressing to her how he really felt about her back then.

Lies, it was all lies. All the shit he said to me back then was lies. "You special. You know I'm the only one who really loves you. Yo' momma don't care shit about you." All that shit. So basically, you was payin' to play back then. You used the presents and the dollar bills to pay yo' little hoe.

Dream picked up her purse from off the dresser and unzipped it. She pulled herself away from his clutches and faced him. The sight of him, standing there staring at her with his beady, devilish eyes nauseated her.

"Why don't you get undressed and relax on the bed. I'm gon' go into the bathroom and freshen up," she told him.

"You do that," he responded, rubbing his ashy palms together.

Dream went into the bathroom of the motel room, flicked on the light, grabbed a towel, wet it and filled it with soap. She began washing every part of her face and neck he had touched. Her mind went back to that day in the tub... the pain, the harsh words he spoke to her afterwards... the blood.

Blood fo' blood, muthafucka!

It was where it all had began for her, the moment that had sent the ball of her life, in a downward spiral, rolling uncontrollably down the hills of destruction.

Where the fuck does he get off, ruining my life and then talkin' to me now like I'm some fuckin' dog? This shit stops here, it stops now and the only muthafuckin' way to ensure that happens...

She pulled out the gun from her purse and rubbed it across its side.

Is to unload into this muthafucka until he got no mo' breath to talk.

Dream cracked open the door and called out to him. "You ready, Ernest? You ready fo' yo' little hoe?"

Ernest was lying on the bed, fully naked and playing with his jimmy. His mind and body were excited at the thought of entering inside his prey once again. He had missed the power he had over her, the way he felt she needed him and would do anything to make him continue to love her.

"You damn right I'm ready, baby! Come on out and show me what you got fo' me."

Dream stepped out of the bathroom, gun cocked and aimed at directly at him.

Ernest's eyes jumped wide when he saw the piece in her hands.

"What the fuck is that? What the fuck is goin' on here?"

"You know what the fuck this is, nigga. It's called payback, muthafucka. Payback fo' every fuckin' thing you did to me."

"Dream, baby, I love you, I always have. Who was there fo' you when nobody else was? Who was the only person that acted like they cared? It wasn't yo' momma, it wasn't yo' sisters, it was me."

Dream's eyes narrowed in on the mouth that was speaking a ton of bullshit.

"You loved me, huh? Well how come you didn't tell my momma the truth that night she caught us? How come you told her it was all my fault? You let her put me out and you don't know the fuckin' hell I've gone through since. You took my family away from me, you son-of-a-bitch! You took everything away from me! No playing outside with the other kids. No bike riding 'cause my pussy hurt so bad I couldn't sit down on the seat. On punishment all the time 'cause you fucked up my bladder when you fucked me and I pissed in the bed constantly…"

"Now don't blame that shit on me! You was pissin' fo' I came along. That's why you was always in the house in the first place," he commented.

"This ain't the muthafuckin' time to be gettin' smart. It was you, *you!* You took my momma away from me. And because of that I lost my baby. My baby was my life, my everything, and because of you, she's gone. So what do you think I should do about that? Huh?"

Dream walked closer to the bed.

"Funny how you ain't got much to say now, nigga."

She paused.

"I tell you what. We gon' play a little game, aight?"

She reached down on the floor and removed Ernest's belt from his gray slacks. She threw the belt onto his chest.

"Tie yo' right arm to that bed post, tightly."

"What?"

"You heard me, tie yo' damn arm to that fuckin' bed post!" Dream shouted.

Ernest took the belt from his chest and rolled over the right side of the bed. He looped the belt around the post and then placed his right arm inside. He pulled the loop tightly and Dream walked over, and with one arm, tied the belt into a knot.

"We gon' play a little game. It's a game of revenge," she said.

"Revenge? Revenge, fo' what?"

You gotta fuckin' be kiddin' me, right? She thought.

"You wanted it just as much as I did. Maybe even mo' than me!" he said to her.

Dream jerked her neck and stormed over to him, pushing the gun up under his chin.

"Fuck you! I was nine-damn-years-old! You think I wanted to get fucked at nine-years-old? You fuckin' pervert! You used me, you used me fo' yo' own little twisted sickness. Yo' own lil' sick ass fantasies. I know, it was a power thing, right? You got off on fuckin' the helpless. Nutted at the thought of fuckin' up a little girl's mind. Well, how does it feel? How does it feel to be helpless, powerless? How does it feel to be the victim of somebody else's twisted shit?"

Dream chuckled.

"I was pissy, huh?"

She stepped back and pulled down her skirt and panties. She climbed onto the bed and stood over Ernest with her gun aimed at his head. She looked him dead in his eyes as the stream of hot liquid flowed down from her vagina onto his face and chest. She smirked as he twisted his head from side to side, attempting to avoid the golden shower.

"Bitch, you crazy fo' real!"

Dream laughed.

"Well, if I am, you made me this way. What, did you think that what you did to me really wouldn't have an effect on my life? You sent me to hell with gasoline draws on, muthafucka!"

Dream stepped down off the bed, walked over to the dresser and took a seat. She opened the drawer underneath her and propped up her feet.

"So tell me, Ernest, why me? Why not one of my sisters or some other lil' girl? Why you choose *my* life to fuck up?"

Ernest ignored her question. He reached across his body and grabbed the sheet. He started wiping Dream's urine from his face.

Dream jumped off the dresser, walked over to the bed and placed the steel object underneath Ernest's balls. He inhaled a deep breath from the coolness of the gun and Dream basked in the fear she saw in his eyes. She'd never imagined anyone, especially a man, afraid of her. She felt the rush, the same rush she had felt the night before when Cali ate her out… maybe even more.

Dream put the adrenaline rush to the side, because deep inside, she really wanted to know the answer to her question. She needed to know what it was about her, if anything, that made a grown ass man, take away her future.

"I can't hear you. I asked you a question. What was it that made you steal away my dreams and replace them with nightmares? Answer me!"

Still, no response from Ernest was given and that pissed Dream off even more. She applied pressure to his nutts with the gun.

"I'm not fuckin' playin' with you! You better answer me before I--"

"Okay! Okay, aight, I'll answer you," he said, holding his free hand up in the air. "I'll answer you. Just get that damn thang away from my dick." He exhaled once Dream pulled her pistol.

"I'm listenin'."

"Aight, aight. I don't know."

Dream shoved the gun back underneath his jimmy.

"Really, I don't know, okay? You was always at home, locked in the house all the time. Always on punishment fo' this or that. Hell, whether you wanna believe it or not, everythang I told you about yo' momma not givin' a damn about you was true. She had told me too many times what a problem child you was. You was just easy prey, that's all I can say, 'cause it's true."

"Easy prey, huh?"

"Yeah..." he paused. "Easy. Then once I got you, hell you liked it as much as I did."

"That's a damn lie!"

"Bullshit!" he spat out. "You got to the point where I didn't need no presents or money to get that young pussy. You started makin' the moves on yo' own."

Dream jumped in his face.

"I thought I was pleasin' the one person who said they loved me. I didn't want you to leave me, too. But now I see why you didn't stand up fo' me the night my momma put me out. You never gave a damn about me fo' real. I was just another lil' hoe to you."

"A good one too," he smirked.

Dream pointed the .22 at Ernest's chest.

"Grab yo' dick."

"What?"

"You heard me, grab it! It was yo' sorry ass dick that caused you to hurt me all those years. Cost me my home, my family, my baby and my life. Grab it!"

Ernest picked up his limp jimmy and held it inside his hand.

"Now what? Yo' idea of revenge is to make a muthafuckin' man play with his dick? I told you, you liked it, didn't you?"

"Fuck you!"

"Yeah, fuck me. You want to don't you? Just like you wanted to back then. You really wanna know why I chose you? That's why I chose you. I could tell you was nothin' more than a lil' hoe, lookin' fo' a dick to put in yo' mouth. And guess what? You still are, ain't you?"

Dream's finger grew itchy on the trigger.

"Ain't you? Look at you. You can't even hold the gun straight. Yo' mouth standin' there waterin' at the thought of puttin' this in yo' mouth. So, why don't you put that fuckin' gun down, be a good little hoe, get over here and do what it is you do best... suck my dick!"

"You go to hell!" Dream screamed as she closed her eyes and pulled the trigger. She let off two rounds instantly.

The gun fell from her hands as she covered her ears from the noise the gun made when it went off. She was afraid to open her eyes and see if she'd hit her target. But when Ernest didn't make a sound, she knew she had.

Blood was everywhere--on the wall, the headboard, the sheets and Ernest. His eyes were wide open as the blood oozed from his mouth.

Dream looked down at the middle of the bed. His hand was still wrapped around his jimmy. She put her finger on the half-dollar-sized hole she'd blown in his chest. She rubbed the red liquid between her two fingers and placed it in her mouth--the taste of sweet revenge.

She couldn't savor the moment long as panic soon started to set in and Dream's pulse began to race. She knew someone had heard the shots and probably called the police.

She scrambled to put on her pants and her skirt. She ran into the bathroom, grabbed the washcloth and wiped her fingers, threw the towel onto the floor and snatched her purse. She went back into the room and put the gun back inside her pocketbook.

Dream frantically searched the room for any sign of her presence, and when she couldn't find anything to indicate she had been there, she headed for the door, not before she turned around once again and looked at Ernest.

"Blood fo' blood!"

She opened the door to the motel room and peeked out in both directions. When she saw that the coast was clear, she took off running across the parking lot onto Grand Ave. She continued to run north towards Natural Bridge and finally ducked into the Church's Chicken along the way.

She tried to act as if nothing was wrong, but when she tried to order her food, she stuttered. When she tried to pay for her food, she shook, and when she sat down at the table watching the police cars fly by, she thought she'd die.

Dream remained inside the restaurant until she saw the Grand bus coming northbound a block away. She ran out the door and across the street to board the bus. She was fumbling while trying to place her fare inside the coin machine. The driver looked at her like she was crazy. When she finally paid her fare, Dream walked to the back of the half-empty bus and took a seat.

Her heart continued to race as she removed a tiny white piece of paper from inside her purse. As she stared down at the contents, Ernest's words burned in her mind:

"…Be a good hoe and get over here and do what you do best, sick my dick…"

Dream removed an ink pen from her purse and marked a line through his name. Ernest was officially off her list. She stared down at the other three names and made it up in her mind that they too would see her soon.

Yes, Ernest had it right about one thing. She was a hoe, had been all her life. But now she was a hoe that could kill.

Chapter Twenty-Two

Garvonni sped down Grand Ave. and turned abruptly into the parking lot of the Lisa's Motel. The motel was rundown and dirty. It was built right next to the corner liquor store and directly across the street from a nightclub called, Club 54.

The motel was known for being one of the hot spots for prostitution because of its location and accessibility. Many calls had come through his dispatcher concerning disputes and domestic violence at the location, so Detective Williams wasn't the least bit surprised he was being summoned there again. He would soon find out though, that this call would be like no other he had experienced at the motel.

He exited the car and headed to the taped off motel room to meet his partner, James.

"What do we got?"

"Man, you wouldn't believe this shit. In all my years of being on the force, I ain't never seen no shit like this. If it wasn't fo' the fact that somebody lost their life, this shit would be hilarious!"

"So you mean to tell me that there's actually a dead man in that hotel room holdin' his dick in his hand?"

"Holdin' it tighter than Oprah's ass cheeks clutchin' a thong," James chuckled.

"You bullshittin'!"

"Nope. Come on, man, tell the locals to secure the scene and let's get to work."

Garvonni followed James and the crime scene investigators into the motel room. When he stepped inside, he had to catch himself because he almost laughed at the sight of the dead man lying on the bed.

"Damn man! I seriously thought you was just fuckin' with me. This nigga's actually laying here tied to a bed post, holding his dick."

"And the kicker is, the muthafucka is still hard. I didn't know rigga could set in like that."

Garvonni held up his finger to his mouth. He didn't want his partner clownin' too much among their colleagues. James could make him bust the stitches out of his pants if he turned him loose.

"So tell me what you got fo' me so far," Garvonni asked James.

James pulled out his yellow note pad from his shirt pocket and began telling Garvonni everything he'd gathered from the staff and witnesses so far.

"Well, the call came in, as you know, while I was talking to you on the phone around eleven. Couple in the next room say they heard two shots ring out and called it in to the front desk, who in turn called 911. Room was registered to the victim, paid up for two hours and the hotel clerk said he checked in with a young woman. She looked to be in her early twenties, around 5'5, one hundred forty pounds, long length hair, and wearing a white top, a blue mini skirt and white tennis."

Garvonni looked stunned as he read off the description of the suspect. It sounded just like the APB he'd put out a few hours earlier on Dream.

Damn, that sounds awful familiar! But that couldn't possibly be her. Not in the shape she was in last night. She couldn't possibly have had the strength to hold his big ass down and tie him up.

Garvonni dismissed the thought as quickly as it came to him. He couldn't find any reason in his mind and in his heart to think that something like this was in her to do, let alone pursue her as a suspect.

She's too frail, too fragile to hurt anyone like this.

But from the looks of the scene, it was obvious that it was an act of prostitution that had gone wrong.

"Did you check his pockets?" Garvonni asked his partner.

"Yeah, everything seems to be there. The motive couldn't have been robbery, he still had over three-hundred dollars in his wallet. His ID identifies him as one Ernest Barber. LKA, 8246 Garfield. We put in a call but we haven't reached the next of kin as of yet."

James walked over to the bed and looked down at the body. The blood flowed from his chest and down his side to the right. That helped Garvonni notice the wet stains on both the pillow at the top of his shoulder blades and the left side of his body. The yellowish color told them exactly what the liquid was.

"Damn, she pissed on the nigga!" James chuckled.

"Looks that way, huh? For this type of shit, I ain't surprised. It ain't uncommon fo' these people to give each other golden showers. Some of 'em like it like that."

"Well, some of 'em a whip damn fool! I wish a muthafucka would try or even ask to piss on me. I tell you what, they'll never piss again. Not through that hole anyway."

"Well, nigga, as both yo' partner and yo' friend, I'm glad to hear you say that, 'cause that's some nasty shit."

Garvonni hit James on the chest and walked over to the restroom to remind the CSI officers to bag up the bloody washcloth for evidence and to make sure they left no stone unturned when dusting the room for fingerprints.

"We can run them through the system and see if we get a hit."

He returned to the room and James.

"So nobody saw anybody leavin' the scene. The only thing we got to go on is the word of an Arab motel owner who probably thinks all black folks look alike."

"Uhh, basically," James responded.

"What about the couple next door? Nothin'?"

"You know black folks' motto: I ain't seen nothin' and I ain't heard nothin'. They feel like they already did their civic duty by callin' it in. Besides, one of them's probably married and ain't tryin' to let it be known they was even at this dirty muthafucka."

"Yeah, I can see that."

"Well, Coroner's here, so ain't really much more we can do at this point other than wait fo' the lab results. You hungry?"

"You treatin'?"

"I got you."

"It's about damn time! If you treatin' then hell yeah, I'm hungry!" Garvonni responded.

"All of a sudden!"

As they exited the motel room, they were met at the yellow tape by a swarm of news reporters. Garvonni held up his hand to quiet the overly anxious reporters.

"All I can tell you right now is that there has been a crime committed at this location. We are working the scene and processing statements from witnesses and when we have something credible to release to the public, you'll all be contacted accordingly."

The reporters asked a few more questions but Garvonni only answered the ones that were really not relevant to his case. He used his words very carefully so as not to put out any unnecessary information.

When he was done talking, he thanked them for their co-operation then he and his partner headed for their car.

James leaned into Garvonni's ear when he saw the coroner passing them with the City Morgue's gurney.

"Aey man, how you think they get that bag zipped up over his dick while it's standin' up like that?"

Garvonni smirked and looked to James.

"You a dumb ass, you know that?"

"I try."

Chapter Twenty-Three

Dream rode the Grand bus until the route ended at the corner of Grand and Broadway. She got off the bus, crossed the street and headed for the Western Inn Hotel located about a block and a half down the street.

When she reached the check in counter, she asked for a room. When asked to present her ID, Dream once again began to shake. She checked into a room on the second floor and paid for a three-night stay. She needed enough time to get her head together and think things through. The last twenty-four hours had not been planned, not to that extent.

Cali and Ernest had just fallen into her lap--handed to her on a silver platter. But even still, Dream had no intentions of harming them at the time. It was just that they had pushed her to the point of no return. Degraded her to her face nonetheless and made her feel like she was good for nothing else but what was between her thighs.

She felt that she had been backed into a corner, and whenever she was harshly reminded of the road that had led to her present condition, especially from the ones who caused it, Dream felt she had to come out swinging. She had only wished she had felt that way along time ago. She wished she had the defensive strength to fight them all both physically and mentally while growing up.

What's done is done. There's nothin' I can do about it. This just must be the way my life is supposed to be.

Dream placed her key in the lock and opened the door. She threw her purse down onto the bed and plopped down beside it. She grabbed the remote and turned on the TV. The midday news was broadcasting the news of a late-breaking story about the murder:

"...We have just been informed of a shooting on the city's north side. Homicide Detectives say the victim was shot to death at

the Lisa's Motel on North Grand Blvd. Police say they responded to a call dispatched through 911 from the owner of the motel around eleven this morning.

The victim's identity is being withheld pending notification of the victim's family. The shooting is the latest in a string of violent crimes on the city's north side this year.

Police are searching for an African American female suspect, early twenties, around 5'5 in height, weighs around 140 to 150 lbs., black hair and wearing a white T-shirt and a dark blue mini skirt. She was last seen checking into the motel with the victim.

If you have any information on this case or know the identity of the suspect, police are asking you to call the Crime Stoppers hotline at 444-4000…"

Dream felt her stomach tighten, her breath shorten and her throat swell. She ran into the bathroom and knelt down with her head buried inside the chilled white toilet bowl. She threw up everything she'd eaten as the tears rolled down her face.

Standing, she turned on the cold water from the faucet and filled her palms. She lowered her face into the cool liquid and tried to stop her stomach from cramping.

Dream looked into the mirror, and for the first time in her life, the reflection was that of a person staring back at her that she was afraid of.

What is happening to me? What have I become? All I wanted was a normal life. I didn't ask fo' this, I didn't. They forced me, they forced me! He called me a hoe to my face. Said it was all I ever was. He shouldn't have done that. A hoe ain't what I wanted to be.

The tears were coming down freely from her eyes. She went into the bedroom and sat down onto the bed. She wiped her face and picked up her purse. Dream removed the gun and laid it beside her on the bed, then she reached down in an inside pocket and pulled out a folded picture.

The tiny face brought the tears to a dramatic downpour. It had been months since she'd held her baby.

Months since she'd seen her smile or had been able to soothe her when she cried.

Dream constantly wondered where Destiny was, how she doing and if she was being cared for in the right way. But above all, Dream often wondered if Destiny was safe. The thought of someone harming her child, touching her in an inappropriate way was more than Dream could handle.

She couldn't imagine her baby girl growing up in the same kind of hell she had gone through, being subjected to people's sick and twisted ways. It was often the reason Dream drugged herself so heavily. She tried to self medicate the pain of losing her baby.

She traced Destiny's face with her finger.

I promised you I wouldn't let anyone hurt you. I promised you and I failed you. But it wasn't my choice. I didn't leave you, they took you from me. Maybe it's best too 'cause now I'm not gonna be around that long. But maybe if I still had you, I would've found the strength to make better decisions.

The thought enraged her and once again, Dream wanted revenge.

They cannot take everything from me that was precious, fuck up my life like this and think they gon' get away with it!

She thought back to her description in the broadcast on the news. She needed to alter her appearance and quick. She gathered her things and headed out the door, down the hotel stairway. She was so nervous because she didn't know who had seen the broadcast of her description. She needed a change of clothes. That was her first priority. She thought about walking up Grand towards the motel to the Family Dollar, but decided against it, figuring the police was still probably circling the area.

Instead, she returned back upstairs to her room, called the Allen Cab Company and headed out to the River Roads Mall, away from the city.

She bought a change of clothes, a pair of blue jean shorts and a pink V-neck shirt. She changed in the public rest room and she discarded her old clothes into a nearby trashcan.

She walked out to the main road, boarded the Halls Ferry Shuttle bus, and headed the Hair Salon. She decided it was best to changes her look all the way, and at the Glamour Girl hair salon, she had her haircut down to a short-cropped cut and had her hair died burgundy. To anyone looking for her, she looked like a brand new person.

Dream gathered up all her bags from shopping and once again boarded the bus to return to the hotel. She took a seat at the back of the bus and put on the earplugs to the portable radio she had bought at the mall.

She stared out of the window as the soothing voice over the airwaves read a letter he received from a woman on the "Quiet Storm" program, "Make My Whoa".

In the letter, the young woman explained how she had just gotten out of a relationship where she experienced a high level of both physical and mental abuse. She explained further how she'd lived her life in fear for over eight years but had come to adjust to the vicious lifestyle because she thought it was normal.

The writer stated how she'd watched her father beat her mother her entire childhood. And since her mother had never complained or left him, she had come to accept that abuse was a normal consequence a woman had to face if she couldn't meet the standards set forth by her man. To her, it had become a natural part of love.

She grew up living with the theory that if a man didn't beat her, he didn't love her.

Dream increased the volume in her ears because she could identify with the woman. She too had often felt that if the same type of things, rather good or bad, kept happening to you, it must simply be the way your life was meant to be.

Dream felt the pain in the woman's words, and the words along with her heart was saddened at the thought of all the things women had to go through for the sake of being loved.

But then, the tone of the letter changed. The woman had begun to speak of how a new man had come into her life and had shown her a new way of living and loving. How he'd become her best friend and how he'd taken the time to get to know her for what was inside of her and not for what she had between her thighs. How he'd stayed by her side throughout a battle with cervical cancer, how they were now married and expecting their first child in a few months.

She spoke of how she'd finally felt so blessed to know what real love was and how she'd almost given up hope on ever finding a man to truly love her, unconditionally.

Dream closed her eyes and leaned her head on the bus window. She could only try to imagine what the writer must have been feeling--joy Dream had convinced herself she'd never find; one she didn't feel she deserved. She felt too ashamed of her life to share it someone, anyone.

Who would want me after I've been with so many men? Who would really care about what happened to me? Who cared about someone taking my baby from me? About my nightmares and shattered dreams? No one! And it's too late, anyway. Who would give a fuck about me now that I got..."

She felt a tear roll down her cheek.

I'll forever be known as a hoe. Starting over and trying to erase people's opinion about you is a chance you rarely get. Ernest taught me that yesterday.

The DJ always ended his letter with a song requested by the person who had written in. Tonight's dedication was New Edition's, *Lost In Love.*

As the words flowed through the earpiece, Dream listened to the love ballad and the words smothered her soul:

"...Would you love me, when nights are cold? Would you love me, when I grow old? Would you care, when living's not easy, take me in your arms and say you're there? Would you love me, give me one more chance. Would you love me, try and understand. Would you share, my life and it's music? Show mw in your eyes, that you'll stay with me tonight... I'm lost in love, I can't live without you..."

Dream had gotten so involved in the letter and the dedication, she'd missed the stop for her connecting bus back to the hotel and it was too far to walk back. Instead, she got off at the Halls Ferry Circle.

She pulled her money from her purse to go into the Chop Suey to get something to eat, use the pay phone and call a cab.

She was down to only about forty dollars and she knew that wouldn't last her but maybe, another day. That brought the harsh reality that she would have to hit the streets and make some money. In her condition, she felt a little ashamed but she also knew she had to survive.

As Dream walked towards the red booth at the back of the restaurant to wait on her food, she noticed a face that looked so very familiar to her. They made eye contact immediately and it sent chills down Dream's spine.

The woman rose from the table and excused herself from the group of girls she was talking too. As she approached Dream, she held out her arms to embrace her.

"Ebony?" Dream whispered.

"Yeah, Dream, it's me. How are you?"

Dream looked into Ebony's face.

"Ebony, what happened?"

Ebony looked off at the concrete floor and spoke softly.

"Pieces happened."

"Pieces? He did this to you?"

"My jawbone never quite recovered from the beating the night when I came back to tell him I was gettin' out the game. They tried to set my jawbone back together but it was too much damage. So until I can pay for some surgery, it's gonna be like this."

The left side of Ebony's face hung down lower than the right. Pieces had crushed her jawbone with his foot and had left her with an appearance that suggested she'd had a stroke.

"Yeah, I remember that night. I've often tried so hard to forget it but it was like some shit straight out a horror movie that scared the shit outta me. Used to always threaten us with that shit too: *'Don't end up like Ebony's ass!'*"

Ebony placed her arm on top of Dream's shoulder.

"Fuck him, it's cool. I'm good, girl. Shit is real good fo' me right now. He only got that pissed 'cause *I* made him what he was. He wasn't shit when I met him and I know damn well he ain't clock as much grip when I left his bitch ass. I got up on my feet, started school and had a baby boy with my man. He didn't stop my flow. He tried but--"

"Tried how? That night you mean?"

Ebony grabbed Dream by the arm and escorted her over to an empty table. They sat down across from each other. Ebony reached down inside her purse and pulled out her wallet. She turned to a photograph of a family--her family.

Ebony was wrapped inside her boyfriend's arms while holding her newborn son in the other. As she turned the photo around for Dream to see, she felt a tear roll down her cheek.

"We would've been together two years this April."

"Would've been?"

"Yeah, he was shot in a drive-by one morning, leaving the house to go to work."

"What, he was in a gang or somethin'? Or just in the wrong place at the wrong time?"

"Naw, the kicker is no one was even outside at the time he was killed. And Dream, in my heart I know that Pieces had somethin' to do with it; I just couldn't prove it. It was payback fo' leavin' him and the game. I know it was."

"Naw..."

Ebony nodded her head.

"Yep."

Dream sat back in her seat. If Pieces had done all that to Ebony, Dream could only imagine what we would do to her once he saw her again. She was glad she had taken Cali up on his offer, if for no reason other than her safety.

"But like I said, it's good now. I've met a lot of good people along the way and now life's treatin' me pretty good. Enough about me, what about you? You still workin' fo' Queen B of the escort game?"

Dream looked at her in surprise.

"Damn, how'd you know I..."

Ebony chuckled.

"Just 'cause you leave the streets don't mean the streets leave you, remember that."

Dream lit up a Newport and exhaled a deep breath. In her mind, she wondered what to say to Ebony, what to tell and what not to tell.

Do I tell her all the things that have happened over the last year or so? Do I tell her about my disease? I mean, her life is goin' so good cause she was gutta enough to take whatever came her way in order to get out the game. What ever Pieces dished out, she took. How can I tell her that I was so fuckin' stupid, I allowed myself to not only get HIV but lose my baby in the process. And I definitely can't tell her about the last twenty-four hours.

"Yeah, I'm still with her. Things are going pretty good too. I make descent money and that helps me to take pretty good care of Destiny. You know she stays with my mom now," Dream lied.

"Oh yeah, that's right. You did have a lil' girl. How old is she now? Gotta be about one, right?"

Dream wanted to cry.

"Um-hum, close."

"Good. Well my order is up and I gotta get home. Say, what you doin' later? Me and a few of my home girls are hittin' Emerald City over in East Boogie. You wanna come? I mean, can you get some time away from the game to hang out with yo' girl?"

Dream was excited at the idea of going out. She had never been to a club before. Plus the fact that it had been so long since she'd seen anyone close to family.

"Yeah, I'm down. I ain't been to the club befo', and seein' you again after all this time is definitely a reason to go out and kick it."

"Aight, girl! Well, here's my pager number. Call me later on and I'll swoop by and grab you."

"Aight."

They embraced and Dream smiled a heartfelt smile.

"Eb, it really is good to see you. I want you to know that I never had any hard feelings towards you, aight?"

Ebony smiled in return.

"Aight; call me, okay?"

Ebony left and Dream grabbed her food and headed for the bus stop at the circle. She reached down inside her pocket and took out the piece of paper she had folded with Ebony's phone number written on it. Dream stared down at the seven digits and started to rip the paper up into tiny little pieces but she stopped. Instead, she returned the paper to her pocket.

In order to go to the club, Dream needed to make some more money, which meant she needed to hit the streets and handle her business.

There's nothin' wrong with it as long as I use somethin'. I ain't tryin' to hurt everybody, *just the muthafuckas that hurt me. Cali, he was just a casualty of the war,* she reasoned with herself.

Chapter Twenty-Four

Garvonni and James headed back to the main station on Spruce and Clark Street in downtown St. Louis after they had lunch at Playboy's Lounge on North Broadway Ave.

When they reached the VCD unit, Garvonni had a yellow sticky note attached to his desk phone stating that the crime lab needed to speak with him. His CSI analysis was back.

News from the crime lab division wasn't good. None of the prints or the DNA that the technicians had collected at the crime scene matched any of the ones in the state or federal databanks. Which meant they had virtually nothing to go on.

Garvonni massaged his temples and frowned. It wasn't because his case had stalled. After all, this was the STL and not only did murders and violent crimes happen everyday but they often go unsolved.

Garvonni was stressed from worrying about Dream. He hadn't gotten any word back about her whereabouts and that wasn't a good sign. To him, that meant she wasn't out walking the streets and it worried him that something might have happened to her. Every time he'd seen her, it was because she was hurt at the hands of someone, including herself.

That bitch betta not have hurt her in any shape, form or fashion, he thought to himself, meaning Kam.

Then he had to realize that Dream was a survivor and that she was bound to go back to what she knew.

Maybe she went to see her kid. She's bound to turn up somewhere. The streets will be calling her soon, and since the streets is all she knows, she's gonna answer.

James hit Garvonni on the arm and told him not to trip. "We'll catch 'em, we always do," he joked.

"Yeah, right," Garvonni chuckled.

"Aey man. Let's go have a drink or somethin'. It's my treat again."

Garvonni looked to his friend.

"You shol' been treatin' a nigga a lot in the last few days. You rob a muthafucka or somethin'? IA (Internal Affairs) ain't gon' come lookin' fo' yo' ass, is they? 'Cause I'm tellin' everythang! Where you live, where yo' momma stay, where yo' hoe on the other side of town stay, all that," he said, touching each individual finger to stress his point to his partner.

"Very muthafuckin' funny! You dry snitchin' now? I knew you wasn't from the 'hood," James snickered. "Naw, I just finally got that bitch up off me with that fuckin' child support. A nigga can breathe a lil' now."

"Damn, how you pull that shit off?"

"This Jewish ass lawyer and a lot of fuckin' grip, you hear me?"

"I hear you."

"So what's good? You down fo' a shot or two?"

"Let's do it," Garvonni replied, dappin' up with his partner.

On the way to the car, their radios went off.

"Oh shit, here we go again! Who got fucked up now?" James asked, turning up the volume on his radio.

"Ten-5, dispatch, be advised I need to be patched through to VCD lead Detective Williams."

"Ten-4, 63…10-12 (stand by)," the dispatcher responded.

"Ten-68 (dispatch information), dispatch requests 10-20 (location) on Dectec--"

Garvonni cut into the dispatcher's message.

"Ten-5, dispatch, this is Detective Williams. Have the officer switch over to channel three."

"Ten-39 (your message is being delivered), be advised, 26. Switch over to frequency three. Detective Williams is 10-12 (standing by)."

Garvonni turned the knob on the top of his radio to the frequency he requested.

"Go for Detective Williams."

"Yeah, Detective, I think I have a 10-99 (possible ID) match on your APB. I got a female fitting the age range, height and weight getting into a green four-door Taurus on Delmar, heading eastbound towards Sarah. She the passenger is in the car with a black male, age range forty to fifty years old. Looks to be a 647 (ongoing act of prostitution) in progress."

"Ten-4 26, I'm 10-76 (enroute) to your location. Permission to 10-26 (detain the suspect). My 10-77 (estimated time of arrival) is about nine minutes," Garvonni said, jumping into his Lumina and starting the engine.

"Ten-4, clear."

Garvonni hit the button on his radio and turned up the volume on his car stereo.

"Aey, GW, for real, what is it with you and this girl? You act like somebody just called you and told you they saw a nigga creepin' out yo' back door with all yo' shit," James said.

"It's deep. You wouldn't understand," Garvonni responded.

"Shit, it must be! Betta be careful 'bout that deep shit, especially if yo' ass can't swim too good."

Garvonni rounded the corner onto Delmar Blvd. and pulled up behind the cruiser that had the two occupants detained inside the vehicle. He removed his side arm and handed it to James.

James in return looked at him as if he'd lost his mind.

"Man, what is you doing?"

"I don't wanna scare her."

"Nigga, is you sure you ain't hit that befo'? You awful sensitive to her needs and shit."

Little did James know that he had hit it before, against his will. As it had been for the past two nights...

...Garvonni pulled the female suspect's hands behind her back and placed the cuffs on her wrists. She winced slightly at the tightness of the iron against her skin.

"What you takin' me in for?"

"You'll see when we get there."

He opened the rear passenger side door to his police cruiser and pushed her head down to help into the car. He walked around to the driver's side door and started the car. He put the car in gear after he adjusted his rear view mirror so he could easily take in her beauty.

He glanced to the rear of the car to find her staring out the window. Then she turned and they made eye contact. He felt a tingle shoot down his spine and he looked away. She liked that and she smiled to herself.

He turned on the radio to get his mind of the lovely creature in the back seat. He also needed to calm the blood flow rushing to the middle part of his body.

The music didn't help much, for neither one of them. The lyrics were seductive and the melody was intense:

"...It's getting' late, why are you still here girl? Have you made up your mind? You wanna make love tonight? I want you to hold me, I want you to be for real girl, please tonight. I want your lips, I even want your tongue love, come give it to me..."

Their eyes locked and held a strong attraction. He applied the brakes and pulled over to a secluded area in O'Fallon Park. She watched him as he exited the car and walked around to open her door. He lifted her out of the vehicle and turned her around, leaning her up against the rear of the car.

She spoke no words of protest. Why would she when she was feeling the same animal attraction? She wanted him just as bad, if not more.

He let his hands slide up her waist and around to her breasts. Slowly, he kissed her on the back of her neck.

"You ready to find out what I got you fo'?"

She whispered in a soft, sexy tone, "I don't care anymore, just use me while you got me."

He reached for his keys on his belt to unlock her cuffs but she stopped him.

"Leave 'em on."

He chuckled. His hands gripped her breasts with force. His tongue danced in and out of her ears. His jimmy was hard and throbbing up against the crease of her ass.

He took his left hand and forced her down onto the trunk of his car while he glided his right hand underneath her skirt. He smiled because she wasn't wearing anything but a navy blue thong, causing her ass cheeks to bulge on each side of the thin material.

He slid his finger under her crotch area to find her mommy already soaking wet. He thrust his finger inside her both forcefully and viciously. The scenic view of her ass and her arms cuffed behind her back almost made him buss on contact.

Her pussy was so hot and juicy he couldn't help but thrust harder and harder with each blow. Her moans excited him, the noise of her mommy popping drove him crazy and the juices glistening off his fingers made his mouth water.

He removed his fingers and raised her up off the trunk. He turned her around to face him. He wanted her to watch him as he placed the fingers he removed from inside her into his mouth one by one.

Her muscles jumped at the sight. She leaned in and stuck out her tongue to enjoy the flavor with him. The essence of her own juices made her clit swell.

He took his left hand and placed it behind her head. He opened his mouth to receive her and allowed her tongue entrance into his. They kissed a passionate kiss, tongues dancing to the rhythm of erotic drums.

He raised up her shirt to find a perky pair of 36C breasts with the nipples sticking out to greet him. He engulfed them into his mouth one at a time while brushing his tongue across them, followed by a cool breeze.

She moaned out in ecstasy, "Um, that shit feel so good, officer!"

He gripped her under her shoulders and lifted her on top of the trunk. He reached around her back, un-cuffed her and threw her back down on the car. He pushed her legs open with force as he looked her in the eyes and said, "I'm a fuckin' Detective!"

He ripped her thong to the side and rushed her clit with his mouth. He tightened the muscle in his tongue and beat it up against her clit. He knew she was near her peak when her legs locked a death grip around his head.

"Who am I?" he asked.

She gripped his shoulders.

"Who am I?"

She wrapped her legs around his arms. He inserted his fingers inside and begun finger fucking her as he savagely raped her clit with his tongue.

"I asked, who the fuck am I?"

"Oooo, Detective! Oooo this shit feels so good!"

He pulled her off the trunk and spun her around. He pulled his jimmy from his pants and stormed it inside her. Burglarizing her mommy hard, rough, vicious and brutal, he pounded against her flesh and she loved it. Her mommy was drenching and he couldn't hold his composure for long. The heat inside her was too strong for him.

She felt him swell and she pulled away. She dropped down on her knees and had his jimmy in her mouth, deep-throating within a matter of seconds.

He became lightheaded. She had the head of his jimmy back at her tonsils, and with the smoothness of her jaws and the wetness of her mouth, his jimmy glided across her throat with an erotic ease.

"Oh, fuck! Damn, baby girl, this shit is fire!"

It was only a matter of minutes before his want for her filled her throat with volume and pleasure. She sucked and sucked until she knew there wasn't a drop left in his sacs.

Then she rose to her feet and licked her lips.

They smiled at each other before she turned back around, placed her hands behind her back and allowed him to place the cuffs back on her wrists.

He helped her back into the cruiser and proceeded to take her back to the same spot where he retrieved her. He opened up the car door, un-cuffed her and kissed her forcefully before he simply walked away.

"Same time next week?"

"You know it!" he said before driving off.

With that, he disappeared…

…Garvonni, now back to present day reality, exited the car and approached the officer's cruiser.

"You run a 10-43 (request for information) yet?" Garvonni asked.

"Yeah, you know how slow the damn computer is though. I'm still waiting."

Garvonni's stomach tied in knots as he walked around to the passenger side of the vehicle. He had mixed feelings about seeing her again. He wanted to make sure she was alright but a part of him also wanted to retreat back to his Lumina because of the kind of thoughts his mind explored concerning her in his sleep.

But he wanted to help her more than fuck her, so he walked up to the side of the door and ordered her to exit the vehicle. Due to his height, he couldn't see the upper body on the female, and it wasn't until she exited the car and faced him that he noticed it wasn't her… it wasn't Dream.

"Damn!" he muttered, pounding on the top of the car. He looked to the young girl. "Get back inside."

He walked over to the cruiser.

"That yo' girl?"

"Naw, but good lookin'. Keep me posted if you get a hit."

"You got it."

Garvonni returned to his car and got inside.

James knew he was disappointed so he spared him his usual wise cracks, but thought, *Damn, I'd hate to see if he ever did get the pussy. This nigga got SP (stalker potential)!* He looked to Garvonni and asked, "You still up fo' that drink?"

"Now more than ever."

Chapter Twenty-Five

Dream had made close to a quick four-hundred and fifty dollars on the streets that night. She made sure to use caution when tricking and even when she gave them service with her mouth, she made them wear a magnum.

She got a ride back to the hotel, showered, changed clothes and called Ebony on the phone to tell her she would meet them at the club over on the east side.

She wore a body fitting, mutli-colored, mid-thigh length dress with a pair of white sandals. She had bought a matching white handbag.

She touched up her hair and put on a light layer of makeup. If you didn't know her, you wouldn't automatically assume she was a working girl. She looked just like any other young girl on their way to the club to kick it and have some fun.

Her Allen Cab arrived just as she was loading her 25 in the bottom of her purse. She wanted to be prepared because she'd never been on the east side of the river and she also didn't know if she'd run into anybody she knew from the streets.

As the cab rolled over the Martin Luther King Bridge, Dream looked down at the water below, then back to the city she left behind. St. Louis was so incredibly beautiful at night, only at night. The glow from the downtown lights glistened on the water and the view of the Arch set it off. Dream wondered how a city so beautiful in vision at night could have so much violence and craziness brewing just inside the city limits.

East St. Louis, Illinois was home to some of the hottest clubs in the Midwest: The Oz, The Broadway, The Pink Slip, The Garrett's, The Max and Emerald City. Collinsville Ave.

was lined from block to block with all types of cars and people.

Dream seemed fascinated by all the people lined up outside the club waiting to get in. She paid the cab driver and exited the cab. As she stood in line, she was flattered by all the whispers and comments she heard as she passed by the fellas.

Ladies got in free until eleven o'clock so Dream eased by the door, smiled at the security guard who was kinda cute and went inside the club. It was dim but it had enough light for her to search out Ebony and her crew.

Dream liked the atmosphere. The club had a main level with the bar, the dance floor, the DJ booth and kitchen. The upper level held another dance floor and a dart room. It was off the chain. The dance floors were packed and the crowd was wall to wall and the music.

Tossin' Ted and DJ Wiz were on the wheels of steel, terrorizing the speakers with MC Breed:

"...This somethin' hard, somethin' funky people gon' dance to. Give the record a second and chance to make you feel who's got the hunger, who last the longest and who's the strongest...ain't no future in yo' frontin'..."

Dream was feeling flow of the club. She liked the way everyone was getting their party on on the dance floor. The crowd was hype, the men were definitely checkin' for her and she was loving all the attention.

The club was so packed she had a hard time seeing two feet in front of her. She searched the scene for a sign of Ebony and her crew but she couldn't find her.

She made her way to the bar and found an empty stool. Within minutes a young man asked her if he could by her a drink. He was so fine to Dream. He had smooth caramel skin color, soft black hair cut into a bob and his teeth laced with gold. He was dressed in a money green Nike sweat suit with white Nike high top tennis. His fingers, his wrists and his neck were blinging as well.

Dream wasn't old enough to drink but he was so cute, she allowed him to buy her a Coke. She was mesmerized by his smile. He seemed so rough, so thuggish and she was even more enthused at the fact that out of all the women in the club, he came over and talked to her.

He had her attention. She was infatuated by him and hung on his every word. His voice turned her on tremendously. The 'hood in him excited her and the way he brushed his hand up against her thigh made her moist between her legs.

"You wanna dance?" he asked her, pulling her off the stool.

Dream didn't answer, she just followed him through the crowd and onto the dance floor. She had never slow danced in her life, let alone actually had a man hold her in his arms. She was so nervous she almost started shaking.

He pulled her close to him, wrapped his arms around her waist and began slowly moving to the music. The Isley Brothers was heating up the moment with erotic lyrics:

"...Why go home to an empty bed, why try to fight the passion in yo' head. We're two hearts on fire, built by a simple touch of love and desire, we both need so much. You're the girl, only girl, so right for me...Spend the night, with me tonight, golden lady..."

Dream almost couldn't contain herself as he slid his hands down her back and onto her ass. She never thought being touched like that could make her knees weak. Usually when she felt a man's hands on her body, it disgusted her.

He leaned into her ear and whispered, "I want you. I wanna spend some time with you tonight, away from all these niggas. Is that gon' be aight with yo' man?"

Dream chuckled.

Man? I ain't got one, never had one, and with all the shit I got goin' on in my life right now, don't look like I'm ever gon' have one. But ain't nothin' wrong with a lil' fun. Shit, he is finer than a muthafucka!

"I don't have a man, I..."

It seemed as if all the music stopped, the dance floor got empty and no one was left in the building but Dream and the man lurking over the shoulder of her dance partner, staring her dead in her eyes.

The man tapped her partner on the shoulder, interrupting the flow.

"I hope you payin' fo' this dance, 'cause this bitch right here owes me a lot of fuckin' money."

It was Pieces, standing in front of her in the flesh with Ebony behind him off to the side. Ebony looked terrified and Dream soon had a duplicate expression on her face.

For a moment, Dream thought Ebony had set her up again, maybe to close out her debt with Pieces but when Ebony mouthed the words, *"I'm sorry,"* to Dream, Dream was certain Ebony hadn't had this one planned.

Pieces had one of his friends standing behind Ebony and when Dream's dance partner saw the size of Pieces' partner, he bowed down and exited the dance floor without so much as a glance in Dream's direction.

So much fo' being a thug nigga, lame muthafucka!

Pieces grabbed Dream around her waist with force.

"You out dancing' and shit? You feel that muthafuckin' cocky about fuckin' me out my money, that you out clubbin' and livin' the high life?"

Pieces had hardly changed since the last time Dream had seen him at the Jefferson Arms Hotel the night he had beaten her three seconds 'til her death. He had cut his curl, grew a goatee and put on a few pounds, but for the most part, he still looked like the same young nigga that befriended her in the park that day, the same man she feared most in life.

Dream thought back to what Kam had told her in the van when she picked Dream up from the hospital. *She told me she took care of him.* Dream knew Kam hadn't lied. Dream knew Pieces well enough to know he was greedy and simply trying to stack cash once again using Dream as his pawn in the game.

"I don't owe you nothin'! Kam told me she paid you off already to release me and you took it."

Dream looked down to the floor as Pieces tightened his grip around her waist.

"She could never pay me as much as I could make off you. Look at you, still lookin' good and ripe. I made you, Dream. You wouldn't be shit if it wasn't fo' me. So come on now, make this easy on yo'self. You know we was unstoppable on them streets."

"From what I hear, Kam ain't really tryin' to fuck with you no mo' after you bought the heat to her spot with that OD and shit. So the way I see it, you need me. You ain't gon' be strong enough to stand on yo' own out here in them streets, you never was. How you think I got you in the first place? I know a weak woman when I see one."

Dream felt her spine crawl the more he talked. How could he expect her to ever fall for this shit again? Last time she went along with the shit he said out of his mouth, he turned her life upside down, worse than what it already was. Now, here he was again, threatening her in so many words but disguising it with slick shit.

Dream knew if she put up too much of a fuss about it and he eventually got her alone somewhere, his next move would be to beat her senseless until she bowed down. So she decided to play the game his way and let him think she was still the young, naive little girl he controlled and turned out years ago.

"You still beatin' on girls?" Dream asked him, forcing her body to relax so he would loosen his grip in return.

"Naw, it's a new way of pimpin' out here now, baby. It don't even take all that. I gotta new way of doin' shit now," he told her, putting emphasis on the last sentence.

Yeah, his plan is to fuck me up, she thought to herself, thinking of Ebony's jaw. *But it ain't goin' down like that. You won't get that shit off me again.*

She thought of Ernest and how she'd felt the satisfaction of seeing him lying on the bed, bleeding to death. Nothing could be more satisfying for her than to see Pieces in the same way. *Blood fo' blood,* she told herself. She thought back to all the times he used her as his punching bag, the heated tip of the gun he used that night to burn the inside of her flesh and all the times he used her as if she was nothing more than a personal toilet bowl to him.

She asked him, "Don't you even wanna know if I still got it? I mean times change, people fall off their game. How do you know I can still bring in the cake if you don't sample my skills?"

Pieces smirked and boasted to himself.

I still got this bitch's mind. She so fuckin' stupid! She got no idea what I'm about to do to her ass.

Pieces was now out of the pimpin' game on the streets and now full fledged into the porno game. He would go to all the local clubs, find some young and desperate girl, buy them a few drinks, take them to his house where he had a studio set up in Dream's old room. There he would drug them and then film them having X-rated sex with not only himself, but all his friends. Then he'd sell them on the black market.

The unsuspecting women would have no idea of the things they had done the night before. After he made the tapes, Pieces always had the courtesy to dress them and lay them in his bed. When they awoke the next morning, he would be lying next to them, fully clothed as well, making the women think he was the perfect gentleman the night before.

Dream was once his star and he planned to use her to his full advantage. He already had half the job done; he didn't need to run game and buy drinks. The mere fact that she was scared to death of him, or so he thought, insured him she would go along with whatever he commanded. But he had a back up plan, just in case.

Both of them had plans and both wanted to come out on top. It was now time to see which one would feel the power. Pieces was sure he had the upper hand, but Dream had plans of her own.

Dream and Pieces exited the dance floor with Ebony and his friend close in tow. Pieces had whispered to his friend and told him to get rid of Ebony. He told him that he had his own business to attend to with Dream. The man gave Pieces some dap and nodded his head.

Dream looked to Ebony and Dream reassured her she would be okay.

"He caught me coming in, outside. My friends backed out on me but I still came because I knew you were already on your way and I didn't wanna leave you here by yo'self. But I swear Dream, I didn't tell him you were inside. He saw you on the dance floor."

"It's aight, Eb, I believe you. Look, I'll be aight. I can handle him. Just do me a favor. No matter what happens when I walk outta that door, I was here with you all night at the club, okay?"

"What are you--"

"Ebony, *all night*, aight?"

Ebony hesitantly agreed. She didn't know what Dream had in mind but she was afraid for her. Ebony knew all to well the wrath of Pieces. She touched her jaw and spoke softly.

"Dream, be careful. Don't do nothin' stupid. He'll kill you. Don't let him outta yo' sight either. I hear he's into druggin' girls now and makin' tapes of 'em, so don't drink nothin' he give you, aight?"

"Trust me, Eb, I'm gutta."

Ebony watched as Dream followed Pieces to the exit of the club. Little did Ebony know it would be the last time she would ever lay eyes on Dream, but not in the way you think.

Chapter Twenty-Six

Garvonni and James pulled up to the Emerald City Club in his Lumina and parked across the street from the entrance. When they reached the door of the club, they passed a few patrons leaving the establishment.

They flashed their badges at the security guard and headed inside the door. A man who seemed to be in a big hurry to leave the building bumped James on the arm. He was accompanied by a gorgeous young woman--Dream!

James turned to Pieces and snapped at him.

"Aey man, you might wanna watch where the fuck you goin'," he said, flashing his badge. "Slow yo' ass down."

Pieces threw up his hands and excused himself.

"My bad, man."

Garvonni was so engulfed in backing up his partner, he didn't even notice Dream at first. But she definitely noticed him. She could smell him a mile away. If it wasn't for the fact that she knew he might be looking for her in connection with Ernest's murder, she would've stood there all night long just to look at him.

She felt the inside of her mommy tighten again. She had to get out of there, fast. As she turned to leave, Garvonni turned into her but the change in her appearance threw him off enough that he still didn't notice it was her. With her haircut and her face made up, Garvonni was thrown off. She looked familiar but not enough to realize it was Dream.

As the couple exited the club, Garvonni and James went inside and headed for the bar. They sucked down a couple of Cokes and Hennessey before it finally hit him:

It was her! She just fuckin' walked right by me!

He looked to his partner.

"You won't believe this shit. That was her!"

"Who?"

"At the door with the nigga who bumped you."

"Who?"

"The one I been lookin' fo'. She cut her hair and it threw me off. It was her, I know it was. I just fuckin' let her walk right out the fuckin' door, dammit!"

James looked to his partner like he was crazy and sipped his drink.

"So why change her appearance? What's she hidin'?"

"Nothin', she just cut her hair, man. Women cut their hair all the time."

"So why walk by you? She knew it was you, you ain't changed yo' looks. That don't seem strange to you?"

"Man, why are you so damn suspicious of er'body? Naw, I mean she knew I was probably gon' get on her head again about the shit she does fo' a livin' and she wasn't tryin' to hear it. Or maybe she was too ashamed to say somethin' to me after I just saw her getting' her stomach pumped a few days ago."

James shook his head in disbelief.

"I don't know, man. Shit seems weird to me. All that you sayin' may be true but all you been doin' is tryin' to help her and she actin' like you out to arrest her fo' somethin'. And now that I think about it, now that you say she cut her hair and changed her appearance, I know you don't wanna hear this but do, or do she not closely fit the description of our suspect at the motel?"

Garvonni looked at his partner like he'd gone flip damn crazy.

"What? Her? Naw, naw, man, it ain't her. She ain't got that in her. Naw, you way off base on that one."

James set his drink down.

"GW, I'm a ask you again. What is it with you and this girl? You trippin'. I mean it's not like the murder wasn't committed in her line of work. And what do you really know about her, besides the fact that her pimp used to kick her ass and the bitch she was stayin' with drove her 'til she wanted to kill herself? Okay, maybe that's all the shit that drove her to snap out on a muthafucka."

"If it was any other girl I was talkin' about, you would at least consider the possibility. But with this one, it's like it's personal in some kinda way and it's keepin you from focusin'. Man, all I'm sayin'--"

His conversation was interrupted by screams coming from the back of the club, followed by a frantic stampede running for the exit.

Garvonni jumped off the stool and grabbed one of the girls running by and asked, "What happened?"

The girl was stuttering and Garvonni could hardly hear a word she was saying.

"Calm down! I'm a Detective. Breath and tell me what happened."

"There's…there's a…a girl. A guy shot her in the back hallway…um, back…back by the bathroom."

Garvonni and James told security to empty the club from top to bottom but keep every one they could outside in front of the club. They told them to ask anyone if they saw anything.

Garvonni and James instinctively drew their weapons and headed back towards the hallway to find the girl lying up against the exit door with a single gunshot wound to the chest. It was Ebony.

The blood had completely soaked her white shirt. Her legs were twisted and tangled underneath her body. Her head hung heavily over to the left side and a trickle of blood flowed down her chin.

Once again, Garvonni saw Keisha's face staring back at him and it gave him chills. He looked around, wondering if the suspect was still lurking in the area. When he saw no one, he reached for his cell phone and dialed 911.

He didn't need to check for a pulse on the body. The flow of blood had stopped, which meant her heart had already stopped beating.

James just shook his head.

"Can't even come have a drink without niggas actin' a damn fool."

"What you think went down?" Garvonni asked him.

"Shit, some nigga probably got pissed off 'cause she wouldn't give him no play. You know how it was back in the day. You try to get a gal's number and when she ain't tryin' to hear you, you call her a bitch and roll on. The game ain't changed, GW. The niggas have just upgraded from words to thumpers."

Garvonni looked at him, amazed he could be so insensitive.

"Do you really, be serious with some of the bullshit you let come out of yo' mouth, man? Do you really think a man is that damn deep over rejection that he'll shoot a woman in the chest, in a crowded ass club like this and kill her 'cause she turned him down?"

"Aey, man, this is East St. Louis. These crazy ass niggas over *hurr* will kill a muthafucka in the drive thru at McDonald's fo' makin' him wait to long fo' some fries."

Garvonni chuckled.

"You a asshole, you know that?"

James winked at him.

"I try."

Garvonni went over to the girl, bent down and picked up her purse from off the floor. He pulled out her ID card and read off the name.

"Ebony Harrison. She's from our side of town."

"Yeah, but she got popped on *they* side of town. Which means this shit is out of our jurisdiction. So when Illinois CSI gets here, I'm out. We got enough shit to deal with on our own side of the river."

Garvonni had to agree with that one.

"Yeah, you right 'bout that," he said, thinking back to Dream.

A security guard from the club came back to Garvonni and James, followed by Dream's dance partner from earlier that night.

The muscle-bound security guard ushered the man over to James and said, "He said he thinks he's got somethin' that might be of help to you."

Garvonni looked to the man, shook his hand and asked him his name.

"Uh, I don't really do 5-0 too well. So let's just say it's Mike fo' now. But check it out. I seen yo' girl over there on the dance floor with this big ass nigga some King Kong lookin' nigga. He was hangin' with this lame ass nigga who stepped on the dance floor and took this hottie I was tryin' to hook up with."

"Did he say his name?" James asked.

"Naw, he didn't. Light skinned cat, bob hair cut, looked a lot like Tito Jackson."

James laughed and asked, "What about the girl?"

"Hottie, about 5'5, short hair cut, nice body…you know, the regular."

"I meant, did you get a name?" Garvonni said, sarcastically.

"Or did you get that far?" James asked.

"Hell yeah, I got that far! I'm tellin' you, baby was feelin' a nigga. If it wasn't fo' that big ass nigga 'ol girl back there in the corner was with, shit, me and homie could've handled up. Anyway, I think she said her name was uh… uh… Dream, yeah, Dream, that's it."

Garvonni and James looked to each other.

James pointed his finger at himself and exclaimed, "Who's the man? Didn't I tell you?"

Garvonni looked to the man and asked, "Are you sure she said, Dream?"

The man nodded his head.

"Were the girls arguing or somethin'?"

"Naw, they seemed to know each other. They also both seemed to be scared as hell of the nigga that rolled up on them," he told them.

She maybe next. Fuck!

Garvonni looked to James and said, "Aey man, brief CSI. I'll be waitin' fo' you out in the truck and hurry up man! She could be the next on his list. It explains why she didn't say nothin' to me when she walked by me with him. Wait, wait, *wait!* Hold up a sec."

Garvonni walked back over to their witness and asked him if the guy Dream was with, had given any clue as to who he was.

The man looked off to the left as if he was trying to remember vivid details. Then it came to him.

"Okay, yeah. As a matter of fact, when he first rolled up on me, he said some bullshit about he hope I was paying fo' the dance 'cause the hoe owed him a lot of money."

Damn, it's him! he thought to himself. He walked back over to James and hit him on the arm.

"I really gotta go, handle this."

James looked around at Ebony and then to the Illinois CSI team coming through the door. Then he realized that he'd rode over to the club with Garvonni and was stuck.

"Aey man, how am I supposed to get back home?"

Garvonni ignored the comment, headed out the front door, ran across the street and jumped in his car. All kinds of crazy thoughts ran through his mind concerning Dream and all the terrible things that could be happening to her at that very moment.

For the sake of his own sanity, he had to save her, he had to help her and he had to find out what was going on inside of him where she was concerned.

He hit the bridge back to St Louis, but it dawned on him that he had nowhere to look for her except the stroll. Her last known address was Kam's Escort Service but he knew she wasn't there.

So Garvonni exited Highway 70 at Grand Blvd. and headed South to Washington Ave. He'd stake out all night if he had to, watching all the action and activities until he spotted her.

If that really was the nigga who beat her and put her in the condition she was in the first time I saw her, then she's definitely out here somewhere. He wants that money. Let's hope that buys her and me some time.

Garvonni sat back and got comfortable, turned on the Quiet Storm and lit up a Kool. He laid he head back on the headrest and watched closely as the young girls took their turns jumping in and out of the approaching cars.

The music helped to relax him as he thought Dream's face and how beautiful she looked when he saw her at the club. Her eyes didn't show any signs of fear but he really didn't pay that much attention to her. But in his heart, he knew she had to be out here scared, not knowing what happened to her friend. Not knowing that Ebony was dead.

If only I could have gotten a hold of her, made her trust me; made her know without a doubt that I'm only here to help her.

The Quiet Storm played soothing music but his heart and his mind was in disarray.

"…There's somethin' in yo' eyes, baby. It's tellin' me you want me baby. Tonight is yo' night. See you don't have ask fo' nothin', I'll give you everything you need, so girl don't be shy. Baby come inside, turn down the lights, cause there is somethin' that I want from you, right now. Gimme that honey love…"

Garvonni couldn't fight the feelings he had towards her anymore. Dream constantly stayed on his mind. Yes, he wanted to help her but this was something else. Something about her, commanded his thoughts at night when his mind was supposed to be resting. She danced across it with a powerful two-step.

He often wondered what drove her down this road. What could have happened to her, that was so bad, it sent into the grimy streets of the hoe stroll? Then the thought came to him. If he could get a line on that, he probably could not only find her but gain her trust.

He picked up his cell phone dialed the hospital and asked to speak with the Patient Representative. When the female voice came over the line, Garvonni explained to her that this was an emergency and that Dream could be in danger. He needed to know the name of Dream's next-of-kin. Most people, when they feel as if they're caught up in life or death situation, reach out to those that are closest to them, even if they don't get along. Garvonni assumed it would be no different for Dream.

The Patient Rep gave him the name of Dream's listed next-of-kin, Karen, her mother. Garvonni thanked the woman and hung up the phone to dial dispatch to run a DMV check on Karen for her LKA (last known address).

The projects? Why am I not surprised?

He put the Lumina to the metal and headed to the Darst Webb housing complex to get some help in both understanding and finding Dream.

But little did he know Karen's place wouldn't yield him a word of kindness, a breath of concern or a thought of remorse. Karen's place would only give him more reasons to find Dream… in a way he would have never imagined.

Chapter Twenty-Seven

Dream sat on the passenger side of Pieces' car wondering what move Pieces might make and how he would try to end her life. She was worried about Ebony and hoping that she had gotten out of the club and away from Pieces' friend.

Pieces, on the other hand, was gloating to himself about his plans for Dream.

Once I get this bitch home and subdued, it's on! I know I can get 'bout three or four flicks outta her ass fo' sho'."

Then he reached for his oversized cell phone and called his friend and business partner, Rick.

"Yeah nigga, I need some of them 'feel goods'. Yeah…yeah. Meet me at the spot and come ready to work. I gotta take this other call man, aight…"

His boy from the club was calling to tell him that the job with Ebony was done and he'd be through later on to pick up his money.

"It was well worth it, you hear me? I been waitin' along time to get that off…"

Dream listened intently as she was sure he was talking about Ebony but she couldn't make out exactly what he was trying to say because he had the music blasting.

"The hoes gon' learn to go along and get along 'cause it might help you live long!"

Pieces laughed at himself as Dream put two and two together. He had hurt Ebony in some way but she didn't know how and to what extent. Those words he had just spoken were the same words he had told them when they first hit the stroll and the same words he had told her the night he'd half-killed Ebony for leaving him.

So Dream knew that she would be next. But it wouldn't be as easy as he planned. Dream had her .22 on her and some how, some way, she was determined to come out on top of this. She had lost too much already. And for the most part, right underneath Ernest, she blamed Pieces.

His fierce beatings are what led her to the hospital in the first place. If she hadn't gone to the hospital that night, Kam wouldn't have ever crossed her path and if she had, it wouldn't have been under those circumstances and Dream would still have her baby.

Blood fo' blood.

Her stomach turned as Pieces turned down the familiar block and pulled up in front of the house that had caused her so much pain and anguish. He got out of the car and headed up the front steps to unlock the door.

Dream was close behind, thinking about the chess game ahead of her. She clutched her purse tightly as she entered the living room and he closed the door behind her. He hadn't changed a thing. The house looked just as it did the last time she'd seen it, still eerie as hell.

"Yeah, let's get this party started. Tho' on some mood music and shit," he said, walking over to the stereo. He picked up the remote and hit the tape deck, bumping Intro out over the speakers:

"...If you let me, let me come inside, I'll keep you, I'll keep you satisfied tonight...if you want me, if you need me... Let me, turn down all the lights, I'll make you, I'll make you feel alright tonight...come inside..."

A knock came at the door and Pieces cut down the volume on the stereo and walked over to answer it. In came a tall, caramel complexioned man, about 180 pounds with long hair braided down the back.

He was nice looking to Dream.

He must be the one he was talkin' to on the phone that works fo' him.

Pieces introduced him to Dream as Twelve. Dream asked him what his name stood for.

"You'll find out soon enough," Pieces laughed.

Dream didn't like the sound of that and she was unevenly matched against the two of them. She decided that she needed to get rid Twelve, and quickly. She walked over to Pieces and asked him to speak with him in private. She needed to make this work. She had a feeling that she was about to be in a train wreck and she wasn't down for that.

When Pieces came in to the kitchen, Dream approached him and put her arm around his neck and her leg around his bottom left calf and said, "I thought it was just gonna be me and you tonight. I wanted to give all this to you and only you. Why you wanna share me? I've learned new things to do with my pussy, new ways to deep throat and new ways to make you come, hard. Why you want him to enjoy the fruits of your labor?"

Pieces listened as Dream rubbed her hand across his crotch. Yeah, he wanted her but he wanted money more. So he lied and told Dream that he'd take care of it and walked in the front room and whispered in Twelve's ear.

"Aey man, leave me them pills and then come back and holla at me in about an hour. The bitch is scared and I'm gon' need a little time to relax her, if you know what I sayin'."

Twelve reached in his pocket and pulled out a small plastic bag containing four tiny blue pills of Valium. He gave the pills to Pieces and then agreed to be back in an hour.

When Dream saw him leave, her mind eased a little bit. One on one, she felt she could take Pieces. She sat back on the couch and agreed to have a drink when Pieces offered.

She excused herself to the rest room. Then she remembered Ebony's warning to her at the club:

"Don't drink anything he gives you, he's into druggin' girls and makin' porno's now."

Dream cracked the door, tiptoed down the hallway and peeked around the corner time to watch Pieces break two small pills and pour the contents into her drink. She paid close attention to which glass he had put the drugs inside of so she would know which one to switch.

She walked back into the bathroom and began to pace the floor. She had to find a way to get Pieces out of the living room and away from the drinks. She wrung her hands, wracking her brain and then it came to her. She knew he kept the plunger in a closet in the kitchen. She figured that she could stop up the toilet and that might buy her enough time to run into the living room and switch the glasses.

She removed a large amount of tissue from the roll and dumped it into the toilet so that it would overflow. Then she flushed it and watched as the water rose to the top and onto the floor. She then called out to Pieces for him to come and check the toilet.

When he came inside the bathroom, he sneered and said, "I see yo' common sense ain't upgraded. You still dumb as a muthafucka. Go in the kitchen and get the plunger."

Dream smiled as she exited the bathroom, ran into the living room picked up the two glasses and swapped them. She placed them back into their spots quietly and headed for the kitchen closest.

When she returned to the bathroom, Pieces snatched the plunger from her hands and fixed the toilet. He told her she'd be cleaning up later on but for now, he wanted her to follow him into the living room and have a drink.

He walked over to the table and Dream's stomach tied in knots. She hoped he didn't notice that she had tampered with the glasses. He picked up the drinks and walked towards her. He handed her right one and she breathed a heavy sigh of relief.

"A toast to gettin' back on top of the game!"

No muthafucka, it's a toast to payback!

He crossed his arm around hers and Dream smiled to herself as she took a big gulp of her drink. Pieces grinned as he watched Dream gulp down her drink.

Yeah bitch, it's on!

Chapter Twenty-Eight

Garvonni pulled up into the project's parking lot and got out of the Lumina. He looked around at all the people standing outside, young cats, shooting dice and selling rocks. He walked right past them with his hand on his gun. He wasn't there to bust anybody; he just wanted to be prepared in case they had a notion of trying to rob him or something.

He entered the high-rise building located at 1401 and walked over to the elevator. When he reached Karen's floor he knocked on the door and awaited an answer.

"Who is it? You betta have a damn good reason fo' knockin' on my fuckin' door this damn late!"

Garvonni chuckled.

What a piece of work!

"Police, ma'am. I need to ask you a few questions. Open up."

He heard close to five locks turn and when she finally opened the door, she still had the chain attached.

"What?"

"Hello, ma'am, I'm Detective Williams of the Violent Crimes Division. Can I come inside and speak to you alone fo' a second?" he asked, flashing his badge at her.

Karen frowned at him and asked, "What is this about? And why can't it wait until the mornin'?"

"Cause frankly, ma'am, the mornin' might be too late."

Karen unlatched the chain and opened the door to allow Garvonni entrance to her apartment. He looked around as he entered and frowned. Clothes were thrown all about and dishes were practically overflowing from the sink.

Clean this nasty muthafucka up!

He turned to Karen.

"Make it quick!" she snapped.

"Um, yeah. I'm here concerning your daughter, Dream."

Karen looked at him like he was crazy. *I know this nigga didn't come wake me up out my sleep fo' anything involving that lil' hoe.*

"I don't have a daughter named Dream."

Garvonni raised his eyebrow and pulled out his note pad to double-check his information.

"You don't? They had you listed as her next of kin at the hospital. Am I--"

"Look, Detective, yeah I gave birth to her but I disowned her lil' nasty ass a long time ago."

Garvonni was blown away at that statement.

"Disowned?"

"Let's just say she grew up to be exactly what she wanted to be!"

"You mean a prostitute?"

"A hoe! Get it right, Detective and let's call a spade a spade. She's a *hoe!*"

Garvonni let out a deep breath. He could tell it wasn't gonna be easy getting any help from Karen.

"Ma'am, I don't know any little girls who sit back and say, 'I wanna be a prostitute when I grow up'. Sometimes things happen that force them to--"

"Excuse me!" Karen interrupted. "And just what are you insinuating? I got a total of three girls that came up in this house befo' her. She's the baby and none of them turned out like her. She's the only one I ever had problems out of. I always told her she would end up just like her damn daddy; dead!"

"And why is that?" Garvonni asked, growing more irritated the more she opened her mouth. He knew his time was running out. "I mean, what signs did she show early on? I'm only askin' cause I need to find her and quick," he said, studying the photos on the wall.

He looked at the younger version of Dream, so innocent and so pure.

What could've happened to you? Talk to me, Dream, come on.

Karen ranted and raved about how since her father died Dream had been a handful. Garvonni half-assed listened as his eyes bounced from one picture to the next. Then he froze. His eyes focused and fixed on a picture of Karen and a man. He knew this man. He had seen him recently… dead at the Lisa's Motel. Garvonni felt sick to his stomach. A wave of emotion shot through him.

It couldn't have been…

He looked to Karen.

"Excuse me, um, I don't mean to cut you off but this gentleman right here, he a friend of yours?"

Karen's tone softened immediately.

"He used to be. Somebody killed him a few days ago. We was together about five years or so but things… things were never the same after… after…"

She walked over to the kitchen sink, picked up one of the dirty glasses, rinsed it out and opened the refrigerator. She took out a bottle of Crown Royal and poured herself a drink.

Garvonni was stuck. James couldn't have been right. Yet, no matter how much it bothered him to entertain the thought, it all made sense to him.

She had opportunity. The crime was committed within her line of work, and she had changed her appearance to avoid being caught. The only thing missing, although major, was a motive.

Why would she kill him? She knew him.

He knew Karen knew the answer. He looked back at the man in the frame. He zoomed in on his eyes. The man looked strange to Garvonni--almost, devious.

"So what happened?" he asked Karen.

She gave no response. Garvonni walked over to her and grabbed her by the arm. He had no time to play these games with her. He needed to get to Dream. After what had just gone through his mind, he was no longer sure who was in danger.

"Look, I need to know what the hell happened. Your daughter's life depends on it. Now tell me what the fuck happened! Did he do somethin' to her? Is there any reason you can explain to me why your daughter may have wanted to hurt him?"

Karen got highly pissed off at Garvonni's tone. She snatched her arm away from him and snickered.

"What the fuck do you mean what did he do to her? The way I saw it, she was lovin' every minute of it! Imagine, comin' home and findin' yo' fourteen-year-old daughter fuckin' yo' boyfriend. Ump and the lil' slut had the damn audacity to say he was molestin' her over the years. Bullshit! The lil' hoe! And I hope she burns in hell if she--"

Garvonni was heated by now. He wanted to slap Karen's ass all across the room.

"You mean to tell me your baby daughter told you a nigga was molestin' her, you saw it fo' yourself and you still didn't do nothin' about it?"

Karen threw her hand on her hip.

"Oh I did somethin' about it. I threw her triflin' ass out in the streets!"

"And kept the nigga, I see."

Garvonni was so mad he had to laugh. *No wonder she wouldn't call yo' dumb ass.*

"Ma'am, do you know where she hangs out, a last address or anything?"

"Tonya? Tonya!"

Dream's second oldest sister came into the living room wearing her bathrobe and house slippers holding her huge stomach. She looked as if she was about to drop any minute. She favored Dream from head to toe but was about five inches taller. She walked over to her mother and stood beside her.

"This here detective is here 'bout yo' sister," Karen informed her.

Tonya looked at Garvonni and displayed genuine concern for her baby sister.

"Is she alright? Ain't nothin' bad happened to her, did it?"

"I'm not sure," Garvonni answered. "That's why I need yo' help. I need to find her. She might be in danger. Can you think of anywhere she might be?"

Tonya thought back to the last time she laid eyes on Dream. Dream was all of seven months pregnant and still staying with Pieces. Dream was leaving the clinic at Homer G. Phillips when she ran into Tonya who worked as a lab assistant on the lower level. When Dream saw her, she almost fainted...

"...Tonya, Tonya is that you?"

Tonya looked at her young sibling and her heart sank. Dream looked as if the world had kicked her ass with concrete shoes on. She had a black eye, a busted lip and a couple bruises on her arms. Tonya's eyes watered as she thought of the young girl with pigtails always coming in her room and following her around when she was younger.

Yet, as Dream got older, Tonya noticed she became withdrawn and stayed to herself a lot. Dream always played in her room and with her imaginary friends, in her own imaginary world.

She displayed a lot of anger at her dolls and Tonya will never forget the day she walked in and saw Dream forcing her female doll to have sex with her male doll.

The language she used told Tonya that Dream had heard it before and had been used towards her, in some way. But Tonya was only a few years older than Dream and when she would mention Dream's behavior to Karen, Karen would just shrug her off.

Tonya felt bad now that she was older but still incapable to move out on her own and allow Dream to come and stay with her. She sat up many nights worrying about Dream. What was happening to her? What was going on with her in the streets?

Now here she was, in the flesh and Tonya's heart broke in two. "Dream, I am sooo happy to see you! I have been worried about you so much! What happened to yo' face?" Tonya asked her, rubbing Dream's belly. "And what is this?"

Dream fought the urge to fall into her sister's arms and cry. She couldn't let her know what was really going on with her. She loved her sister, but deep inside she also knew that their mother had poisoned them against her and Dream knew that whatever she said, Tonya would go back and report to Karen.

She couldn't let them know she was being tortured out there on the streets. She couldn't let them know that men all across the metropolitan area were using her body at their own personal disposal.

Dream tried her best to put on a front like everything was going just fine.

"Oh, this. It's nothing. Me and some girl got into it. Her and her friend tried to jump me."

"And this?" Tonya asked, pointing to Dream's protruding stomach.

"You know how it is. Shit happens sometimes out here."

"You with the daddy?"

"Yeah," Dream lied. She really couldn't tell her that she had no idea who her baby's father was because the baby was a product

of the stroll. "We doin' good too. I'm on my way home as a matter of fact," she said, adding to the lie.

" I can take you. I'm off now," Tonya offered.

Dream hesitated. She didn't want her sister knowing she stayed in a full-fledged hoe house. So she told her sister she'd be alright on the bus and thanked her for the offer.

Tonya insisted and eventually won out in the end.

Dream guided her to the corner house of Washington and Sarah Streets. She politely thanked her once again and told her she'd call her. She was really trying to get back inside before Pieces came home and found out she went to the clinic while she was on his time clock.

"You promise you'll call? Tonya asked, not wanting to leave her sister behind…

Tonya looked at Detective Williams with a tear rolling down her face.

"That was the last time I saw her. I watched her walk in the house and I pulled off. That was almost two years ago."

Garvonni walked over to Tonya and put his hand on her shoulder.

"Don't worry, I'll find her."

He looked to Karen and said sarcastically, "You have a good night."

"Bitch!" He muttered on his way out.

He walked out the door and slammed it behind him. He took the stairs down to the ground level and ran over to his car. He started the Lumina and sped off towards Washington and Sarah.

"I was just there, dammit!"

Chapter Twenty-Nine

About an hour had passed since Dream had swapped the drinks and now much to her delight, Pieces was so out of it. Dream actually had time to plan out the exact way she wanted to torture him. To drag his dead body weight would be too much for her to handle, so she decided to leave him sitting right there on the couch.

She took a seat directly next to him and continued to sip on her champagne.

"You had big plans for me tonight huh, Pieces? You are one sadistic muthafucka, you know that? For as long as I've known you, you've thrived of my weaknesses. You beat fear into me and made me believe I would never be worth nothin' more than what my pussy brought in. Now, you still tryin' to exploit me, just in a different way. Well, guess what? Karma's a muthafucka!"

Pow!

She slapped him forcefully across the face and then jumped back, awaiting his retaliation. When nothing happened, she smiled. It felt so good to hit him, she did it again and again and, ahhh... again!

His body was so weak under the influence of the pills, he didn't know if he was coming or going. Dream tried desperately to use that to her advantage. She wanted him to feel every inch of pain she'd ever suffered at his hands, once he awakened.

She rose up off the couch and stood in front of him. With all the strength she could build up, she balled up her fists and began swinging, punching him from every angle. Each blow was filled with rage and hatred for the part he played in what she'd become.

When she saw his lip trickle with blood, she chuckled. It wasn't nearly enough to satisfy her. She started unbuckling his belt but was interrupted by a knock at the front door.

She ran into the bathroom, grabbed a dirty towel that was hanging from the shower curtain, wet it and came back to the living room to wipe the blood from his mouth. She needed it to appear that he'd gotten drunk and passed out, so she pulled his legs up onto the couch and placed his empty glass on the floor beside him.

She grabbed her purse, walked over to the door, peeked through the peephole and opened the door.

Twelve looked like he'd just seen a ghost when Dream opened the door to let him inside. He expected Dream to be downstairs by now, butt naked and ready for action. Seeing her standing there meant something wasn't right. He stepped around her and looked to Pieces.

"We got to talkin' 'bout old times and he kept chasin' his drinks and I was sippin' mine, so needless to say, he's a lil' bit more fucked up than I am," Dream told him.

Twelve studied Pieces for a minute and Dream started getting a little scared and fidgety. She put her hand inside her bag and grabbed her gun. She just wanted to be on the safe side in case he tripped.

Twelve had never seen Pieces pass out from liquor before, then again, he'd never been around Pieces and Dream together, so he just shook if off and figured that Pieces had just gotten a little carried away since he hadn't seen Dream in a long time.

Dream was relieved when Twelve turned back towards the door to leave. She took her hand off her .22, followed him to the door and gave him a halfhearted laugh.

"You know how he gets sometimes."

"Yeah, just uh, tell him hit me in the mornin' when he gets up."

Dream closed the door and stood peeking out of the curtain in the front room window to make sure that Twelve had left. When she saw him get into his car and drive off, she breathed a sigh of relief. Her heart returned to its normal rate as Dream turned her focus back to Pieces.

She walked over to him on the couch to continue her mission. She unbuckled his black leather belt and began unfastening his Tommy Hilfiger jeans. She wrestled the jeans, along with his solid gray boxers, down to his lower calves.

Dream shuttered as she thought back to the pain she felt at the hands of Pieces. The pain from the burning hot steel he'd placed constantly in and out of her vagina the night Kam took her to the hospital. The blisters, the burning... the smell of her own flesh.

Revenge for Dream would be sweet, as she walked over to her purse on the table and reached inside to grab her .22. Then, she knelt down on the floor beside him, took a lighter from his pocket and heated the tip of her gun.

The aroma of his skin quickly filled the air as Dream touched the tip of his jimmy with the heated gun. She pulled back and again she awaited a response from him. All that was able to come out of his mouth was moaning and groaning. Dream again heated the tip of the .22 and placed it onto the shaft of his jimmy. Again and again she burned him from top to bottom.

Then she heated the gun one more time, pulling his balls up toward his blistering jimmy to make sure she touched the thinnest part of his nuts. When she found it, she placed the gun against it with force.

Never will you make babies, you bastard! Never will there be another you! Not in my lifetime!

Dream pulled his belt from his pants and stood back, thinking of all the times he'd beat her with an extension cord.

Whoop! Whoop! Whoop! Whoop! Whoop!

She whipped him against his arms, his legs, his chest and the now bleeding, pus-filled burns on his jimmy and balls, like she was his master and he was a deadbeat slave.

This is fo' Ebony!

Whoop!

This is fo' me!

Whoop!

A knock came at the door and Dream dropped the belt.

Please tell me that ain't Twelve comin' back!

There was no way she could let him back inside the house now, not in the shape Pieces was in. He would definitely know something was wrong.

Bam, bam, bam, bam, bam, bam!

What Dream heard next almost caused her to drop dead.

"This is Detective Williams of the VCD! Open up! I know you're in there!"

Dream froze. She didn't know what to do. If she let him in, she'd not only be arrested for what she was currently doing to Pieces but for killing Ernest as well.

How the fuck did he find me? Oh shit, oh shit! I'm in so much trouble… shit!

She became frantic. She paced the floor as Garvonni continued to pound on the door.

"Either your open the fuckin' door or I can get a muthafucka over here to open it fo' me!" he yelled.

His voice rose at the thought of Pieces doing something crazy, like holding Dream hostage. Little did Garvonni know, Dream could stand on her own--that was until he came knocking at the door.

Dream exhaled a deep breath and tried to swallow the lump in her throat. She had to open the door before he came bursting through it. She felt her eyes well up with tears.

I guess it's really over. I'm gon' spend the rest of my life in jail! I'm already sick and shit... fuck! I'll be behind bars for whatever time I have left.

She looked to Pieces.

You one lucky muthafucka! I should've just killed you off the flip! Everything about you just keeps fuckin' up my life!

Dream went into Pieces' bedroom and grabbed the spread from his bed. She threw the cover across his half-naked body and pulled it up underneath his chin. Then she took the empty champagne bottle and sat it by him on the floor.

She put her gun back inside her purse and laid the bag down on the table. She walked over to the front door and unlatched the top door lock. As the door squeaked open, Dream's heart raced when she saw Garvonni standing there, gun drawn and ready for whatever awaited him on the other side of the door.

When Garvonni saw the horrified look on Dream's face when she opened the door, he wanted to drop his gun to his side but he couldn't because he didn't know what Pieces was up to inside the house.

"You alone?" he asked her, climbing two of the six steps to the front door.

Dream didn't respond. She didn't know what to say to him.

"Dream, listen to me, its aight. I just need you to talk to me and tell me if you're in the house alone right now. Nobody's gonna hurt you. I'm out here all myself. I'm here to help you, Dream, but I can't do that if you won't talk to me."

It seemed like *déjà vu* to Garvonni, begging and pleading for Dream to let him inside her world and allow him to help her. The fact that he was there meant that he had already gone too far. He'd gone against department policy by not reporting Dream as a suspect, not calling for backup and for attempting to enter Pieces' home without a search warrant. Garvonni didn't care, he just wanted to get to her and stop anything else from happening to her. Everything else, he would handle later.

"You can say that," Dream muttered.

Garvonni tightened his grip around his gun as he climbed the final four steps and reached the front doorway. He told Dream to step back, slowly. He entered the house and scanned across the room. His eyes fell on the man he saw in the club with Dream, lying on the couch, draped in a blanket and looked to be unconscious.

Garvonni cautiously returned his gun to his side. He turned and looked to Dream who was standing behind him, looking as if she was about to shit on herself.

"You finally wanna tell me what's goin' on?" he asked Dream as he moved in closer to her.

"He just got drunk, that's all. It's nothin', really."

"Really? You mean to tell me that this nigga's hold is that strong on you that even while he's unconscious you still scared shitless of him?"

"I'm not scared of him. I'm not scared of nobody... not no mo'!"

"So what happened here, Dream?"

"Nothin'. I told you he just had a little too much to drink and I--"

"A lil' to much, huh? Like Ernest at the motel?"

Dream almost choked on her breath and stumbled back against the wall.

"You know?"

"I know more than you think, Dream. At least at this point I'm assuming some shit but that's why I'm here. I wanna know what the hell is goin' on. You can trust me, Dream. I think the fact that I'm here should let you know that. I didn't bring the cavalry when I found out you were at that motel. I wanted some time--some time to talk to you and find out what really happened. But I need you to talk to me."

Dream slowly eased down onto the couch by Pieces. A quick jerk of his leg caused Dream to jump and Garvonni to once again raise his weapon. But Pieces was still too out of it to do anything, and once Garvonni realized that, he lowered his side arm again.

"I…I don't know where to start. The beginnin' would take to long."

"I'm officially off the clock," he said, removing his radio from his holster and turning the knob to the *off* position. "I got time."

Dream felt the tears roll down her cheeks as she inhaled and exhaled, then began telling Garvonni, line by line, the story of what pushed her to live the life she led.

She told him of her father and how her life had changed once he died. How she felt it was at that point that her mother began to hate her. How Karen began staying out all night, leaving her daughters at home alone in the projects. How Karen gave every man she dated a key to their apartment and left them open to visit any time they wanted, whether Karen was there or not.

"I was the youngest of the group and I don't think she realized that I needed somebody there to protect me. Eight years old and everybody just kinda said fuck it and went their own way. They left me there with him…"

Her voice faded as the tears began to flow.

"What the hell did they think was gonna happen? He used to bring me all kinds of stuff and tell me all the time how my momma didn't like me and always said she wished I was never born."

"The fact that she was never around me made it that much easier for me to believe him. He was the only person besides my daddy and my Nana that ever told me they loved me. My momma just yelled, screamed and hit me. To this day, she's never said, *I love you*, can you believe that?

The first time plays like a Freddie Krueger movie, over and over again in my mind. The blood, the pain…"

Garvonni rubbed his head. It hurt him to hear her talk about the things she'd gone through. Things she didn't deserve to have to feel at such a young age.

"I saw him on the bus that day. Can you believe he didn't even know who I was? Can you believe that shit? You took away from me all I had that gave me identity and you fuckin' forget how I look? He ripped away at my flesh. I couldn't get the vision of the water turning so red from all the blood out of my mind.

The night my momma walked in and saw him fuckin' me, she… she blamed me, not him and she chose *him*, not *me!* She put *me* out! Sent me out into the streets where young girls are preyed upon by every kind of wolf in every kind of sheep's clothin'.

That day, when I saw him, I had just left the hospital after talking to the doctor, thinking my life couldn't possibly get any worse and there he was."

Dream looked at Garvonni for the first time. She looked him dead in the eyes.

"I *made* him remember me, Detective. I made him acknowledge that I existed. But you know what? He couldn't even do that right. He still called me his little hoe and was still talkin' that shit about how I could never be good at nothin' but spreadin' my legs."

She chuckled.

"I guess I showed him, huh?"

Garvonni had just gotten a murder confession from Dream, but he wasn't in a hurry to act on it. His heart ached for her. He wanted to reach out to her, make the pain go away for her. He knew after talking to Karen that Dream was telling the truth.

"And what about this?" he asked her, pointing to Pieces.

Dream looked to Pieces and then to Garvonni. She told him about how she met Ebony and Pieces in the park the day she left the hospital after being put out by Karen and gang raped shortly after. She told him how they offered her a place to stay.

"I thought they were truly offering me some help. Instead, in exchange for a place to stay, I had to sell my pussy out there on the stroll. Yeah, it was him who beat me the first time you came to the hospital. Used the burnt tip of the gun to burn the inside of my shit. Wanted the next couple of hours on the stroll to hurt me that much more as a consequence for losing his money to a trick. But you know what?" she asked, snatching the cover from Pieces body.

Garvonni almost threw up at the sight of Pieces' balls burned and blistered.

"Like Ernest, I made him feel what I felt!"

Garvonni stood up at walked over to Dream. He knelt down in front of her while she was still sitting on the couch.

"Look, Dream, I'm sorry. I'm so sorry for all those things that happened to you. They deserved this, yes, but you have to listen to me. We have got to get this man, no matter how much of a low down, disgustin' son-of-a-bitch he is, to the hospital. 'Cause if we don't, you're gonna be lookin' at another murder rap. Look at me, Dream."

He pulled Dream's face up to his.

"I wasn't the only one who saw you leave with this guy tonight. We gotta get some help. I'll think of something. But we gotta do this, aight?"

He wiped the tears falling from Dream's face.

"Will you let me help you, Dream? I know, I know those men all pretended like they wanted to help you and pretended like they cared about you. But I can help you. You *and* your baby girl."

Dream's sobs became uncontrollable.

"Please Dream…tell me, tell how to help you."

"She's gone… *she's gone!* She took her from me and she's gone!"

"Who's gone?" he asked her, continuing to wipe her face.

"My baby. I haven't seen her since I left the hospital. The day Kamry picked me up from the hospital, she told me that my baby was at her friend's house. She told me she was keepin' her until I got better. But when I kept pushing her to take me to see her, she finally told me that she was holdin' my baby hostage until I paid her."

Garvonni's blood began to boil. He'd asked Kam where Dream's daughter was the night of Dream's overdose and Kamry had lied to him and told him the baby was at Dream's mother's house. *Funky bitch!*

"Paid her? 'Til you paid her for what?"

"My hospital bills she claimed she covered, the cost for her friend that was supposedly taking care of Destiny and the money she said she gave to this muthafucka right here to cut me loose, free and clear."

"That's extortion and kidnappin', Dream. I can get yo' baby back fo' you. I can bring the madam in on felony charges and force her to tell me where she is. But this ain't the way to handle this shit.

Dream, you gotta believe me. I know you got issues when it comes to trustin' people and believe me, I understand. But I'm not them, Dream. I'm not gonna hurt you and I'm not gonna let anyone else hurt you either, that I promise you. But I need you to trust me. Do you think you can do that, Dream?"

Dream looked him in the eyes, looked over to Pieces and back to Garvonni. Her heart told her he could be trusted. Her heart told her to leap into his arms and allow him to make everything better.

But her mind disagreed. How many people had crossed her path and pretended that they gave a shit about her, only to find that they wanted something from her in return.

"Why are you so hell bent on helping me? Everybody's got an angle, so tell me...please tell me, what's yours? I can't do this shit no mo'! If muthafuckas would've just kept it real and put their cards on the table and told me what they wanted from me off jump, I could've decided if I wanted to go through the shit. You know, tell me they wanted to steal my childhood away from me: Tell me they wanted to pimp me out: Tell me they wanted to turn me out: Just tell me!"

Dream was yelling, pounding on the top of her thighs to emphasize her frustration and crying beyond comforting.

"I can't do this no more, I can't! So please, please just tell me what it is you want from me?'

Garvonni sighed.

"I had a friend once, from the 'hood I grew up in. She was a wonderful girl. Her name was Keisha..."

Garvonni felt himself starting to get choked up, so he cleared his throat and continued.

"One day, I was leaving practice at school and I heard some screamin' comin' from the back of the Rec building. I ran towards the screams and there she was, lookin' up at me, beggin' me to help her but I... I couldn't. She was being raped by two of my homies.

Back then, I was deep in the gang bangin' life and... you just didn't turn on yo' homies, no matter what. They ended up killin' my friend that night and I've had to live with the vision of her face in my dreams all these years.

When I saw you at the hospital, I didn't see you... I saw Keisha. And I felt as if it was my chance to make it right, to finally do right by her by helpin' you. At least, I thought that was it at first but it wasn't..."

He paused.

"Can I tell you somethin', Dream?" he asked, placing both of her hands in his palms.

Dream nodded her head.

"I have thought about you every day since I first laid eyes on you at the hospital. All I could think about, was how could anyone, hurt such a beautiful creature. I wanted to help you, be there for you, maybe even save you. You and your baby girl deserved better than what the world had given you and I wanted to help you reach that higher level."

Garvonni rose up from his knees and stood in front of Dream. He extended his hand to her.

"I wanna hug you. I wanna hold you in my arms until you know without a shadow of a doubt that it's a safe place fo' you to be. Can I do that for you?"

Dream looked up at Garvonni and for the first time in her life, she wanted a man to wrap his arms around her. Not just any man, this man.

She placed her hand inside his and with his help, she stood up and leaned into his chest. Her body instantly gave way as his arms wrapped around her. Dream closed her eyes and allowed the tears to flow.

"Its aight, everything's gon' be aight, Dream. We'll figure this out, somehow. Just let it go... let it all go. You're safe now."

Every time Dream inhaled, she smelled him and she loved it. She did just as he had instructed her to do, she let go. Let go of every bad thing that had ever haunted her, taunted her.

The radio in the living room was still playing the Quiet Storm and as Garvonni held her tight. Baby Face expressed to Dream all that he felt inside:

"...But soon as love appeared, you turned away. And you were scared that love, would blow your heart away. And you were certain that, in time my love would stray. So where, where will you go? And who's, who's gonna love you like I do? Where will you go? And who's gonna love you like I do..."

He squeezed her tighter and she felt a tingle shoot down her spine.

She looked up into his eyes and asked, "How is it gonna be okay? I hurt some one really bad. Their gonna send me away for a long time and... and I don't have much time left. I..."

Dream wanted to tell him the worst of her news but she was afraid. Afraid he'd remove his arms from around her; afraid he'd remove his offer to help her.

Garvonni brought his hands to her face and forced her to look at him.

"I'll figure it out, Dream, I promise. I...I just feel so bad for you. I feel so bad because a woman so beautiful as yourself has never had a man to send her flowers. Never had a man take her to dinner, never had a man to... never had a man to make love to her. You know what that means, Dream? It means you've never lived. You've been walkin' around this earth dead inside and I...I..."

He stopped and gave up trying to explain what he felt. Instead, he kissed her, hard yet slow. He wanted her to feel what he was feeling. He wanted her to know that all men weren't scum and that there was one out there who thought of her in a special way.

Dream closed her eyes and fell into his kiss. She had never been kissed like that before and she wished the moment could last forever.

Garvonni ran his hand down her back and pulled her closer to him, making their bodies touch. After all the dreams, all the times she invaded his thoughts, he made her feel it. And she did.

Dream was unsure how to respond to him. She wasn't too experienced in the passion area. But his touch and his kiss felt so right, she let it flow. She slid her hands up his back and gripped his arms tightly. She felt his nature rise against her abdomen and it excited her beyond her wildest imagination. Her mommy was juicy and heated higher than a broiling oven.

He whispered in her ear, "I want you, Dream. I don't care where you've been or what you've been through. I wanna show you how life is supposed to be. Show you how special you really are and how you're supposed to be treated."

He gripped the back of her neck and kissed her again.

"Let me...let me show you a better way."

Dream wanted him so badly but she knew she couldn't have him. She was tainted and she also knew that everything he told her would change once he found out.

This feels so damn good... too good! But I can't do this. I've hurt enough people already. They deserved it, he don't. So I might as well get this over with. Just one more kiss, then I'll tell him.

Garvonni smothered her with his lips and Dream felt the inside of her mommy tighten. He ran across the outer rim of her mouth and she felt her legs shake. Then she pulled away from him.

He said, "I'm sorry! I'm sorry, Dream. I didn't mean to make you uncomfortable. I…"

"No…no, it's not you, it's me. I…I can't do this. Not because I don't want to but because I can't. I've already fucked up my life; I refuse to fuck up yours too. The night you were at the hospital talkin' to me, you know when the doctor came in and asked you to leave? Well, she came into my room to tell me…"

She broke down again.

"She… she came to tell me that I have AIDS. I'm gonna die. I'm gonna die!"

Her legs almost buckled to the ground when she finally said it. To say that out loud made it seem so final.

Garvonni caught her and held her in his arms again.

"Now you see why I wanted them to pay. They have taken everything from me, everything that has ever mattered to me. They stole it and used it fo' their own twisted pleasures. Now they've taken my life from me. What is wrong with me? Why do people keep hurtin' me?"

She sobbed uncontrollably and Garvonni felt his heart split in two.

AIDS?

He felt his eyes well up. He wanted to fix her life but this was one thing he couldn't make better for her. She had been given a death sentence. But instead of freezing up, Garvonni decided he would give her the one gift that time could never erase… the gift of feeling loved.

He looked at Dream and said to her, "Was that supposed to scare me away? I meant what I said, Dream. I want you to know what it feels like to be loved, now more than ever."

With that, he kissed her again with no thoughts of her disease or its repercussions. He wanted her and he was determined to have her.

"Take me to his bedroom."

"But..."

"No buts, just take me."

Dream hesitantly grabbed his hand, led him past Pieces and into his bedroom. Once inside, Garvonni turned Dream to face him and placed a soft kiss on her forehead.

"I'm about to show you how it should feel."

He placed soft, warm kisses on her neck.

"Feel that? That's a good kiss. You feel my hands? That's the way a man is supposed to touch you. Soft, gentle like. No hurries, no need to rush. He's supposed to enjoy every inch of your body. It's so soft, you feel so good..."

Dream swallowed the lump in her throat.

"I do?"

"Take yo' hand and run it down my stomach. You feel that?"

"Yes."

"Feel how hard it is? That's in response to the way your skin feels to me. I've dreamed about you so many nights. This right here, this right here is what I've thought about since I first laid eyes on you. I don't want you to take this the wrong way. I didn't just wanna fuck you, I wanted to make love to you. Explore you, let you explore me. Hold you and caress you like never before. I wanted to be the one to bring a smile to your face and to your heart. Wanted to make you feel all the things I've been feelin'.

I wanted to kiss you. I wanted to feel you, let you feel me. And now that I've got you here in my arms, nothin', you hear me, nothin' is gonna stop me from accomplishin' that."

"You think?" he asked.

Garvonni and Dream turned to find Pieces, standin' behind them with his gun drawn on both of them. He had awakened in intense pain from all the things Dream had done to him earlier that evening.

When he tried to stand, the pain from his balls almost made him pass out again. Dream and Garvonni couldn't hear him moan because of the volume of the radio. He couldn't stand up on his own and he definitely couldn't pull up his pants. So, he kicked off his jeans along with his boxers and tiptoed, gingerly to the recliner, reached underneath the pillow and grabbed his gun.

He heard their voices, faintly coming from the bedroom--his bedroom. He thought that Twelve had come back and gotten the party started without him.

I know damn well, these muthafuckas ain't in my room, fuckin' and shit!

Then he wondered how he had fallen asleep in the first place. It should have been Dream that was out of it from the wine he drugged. He couldn't understand how it had ended up in his system.

That fuckin' bitch! She must've switched the drinks. But how could she have known? Ebony! That country ass bitch must have warned Dream befo' we left the club. It's all good though, that's exactly why her ass is takin' a dirt nap right now!

He stood in the doorway leaning against the door frame watching as Garvonni and Dream shared a kiss. Their passion for one another had them both distracted and had allowed Pieces the perfect opportunity to get the ups on them.

Garvonni positioned himself in a way that Pieces couldn't see him place his hand on his sidearm. He moved Dream to the side.

"I don't know who I wanna kill first. Yo' punk ass fo' comin' up in my shit disrespectin' me like I'm some lil' bitch, or this hoe fo' druggin' me and burnin' my dick!"

"You don't wanna do this. You don't know who you fuckin' with right now," Garvonni warned him.

"Naw, muthafucka, you don't know who *you* fuckin' with! I run these streets over here! This here's *my* block! That there's *my* bitch!" he screamed, pointing the gun at Dream. "And this bitch needs to be taught a muthafuckin' lesson! Don't no hoe cross me, no hoe! Ya friend Ebony learned hers earlier tonight. I guess it's yo' turn. I always said the best hoe; is a dead hoe!"

"He killed Ebony?" she whispered, looking to Garvonni.

"Bitch is deader than Harriet Tubman! And you two bitches can build an underground tunnel together 'cause you 'bout to die too!"

Pieces cocked his gun... Garvonni drew his... Dream shut her eyes tightly as the shot rang out... the blood splattered... a chest opened... a breath shortened... the scream's mounted... the eyes closed... *damn!*

Mimika Avenue

"You Must Respect The Game…"

Prelude

Seven am on one of the Walnut Park neighborhood's hottest mornings, Man stepped onto his discolored brick porch with his arms stretched wide, inhaling the smoggy air of Mimika Avenue. He pulled up one of the off white chairs, reached in his pocket, pulled out his cigarettes and lit up a Newport.

Man was Walnut Parks' neighborhood version of Martin's *hustle man.*Any and everything you could want or need, he could get it for you. Need a TV, call Man. Need a transmission for your car or an air conditioner for your crib, call Man. Need gun play; you could call him for that too.

Standing all of five-foot-two inches tall, one hundred and twenty pounds, dark-skinned, with medium length braids and two fang style gold teeth, Man was a handful with the ladies.

The neighborhood *chicken-heads* flocked to him like flies to shit, but Man was a business man and he heavily believed in MOB (Money-over-bitches). He never put anyone before his money, especially a piece of pussy.

Man was an all around good guy from the hood. He'd help you out if he could but if you should so happen to get on his bad side, look out. He had mad artillery and he was down for poppin' his nine when necessary.

As he puffed his nerve relaxer, Man called out to the local neighborhood dope man as he exited his '04 tan and chrome Suburban truck across the street.

"Aey nigga! It's time fo' that medication."

"It's good my cat, just gimme one sec, I got you," the man answered, turning up his favorite liquid beverage, an ice cold tall can of Bud Light.

Spider was everybody's favorite herb specialist. He had the fattest bags around and he always believed in sharing his wealth with those closest to him.

Standing five-eleven, two hundred and twenty five

pounds, mocha complexed with broad shoulders, Spider was hood to the bone. His braids, long in length and designed in the latest styles. His calf-length Phem shorts starched fresh from the cleaners and his thigh length white tee, creased sharply down the center. His legs were slightly bowed and sported his war wounds of the past. His arms, flossing the tattoo's of the Laclede Town set he claimed as a youth.

Spider walked onto the porch of the run down, one family unit located at the corner of Mimika and Harney Avenue. He sat down his Bud Light and gave hood love to his home boys, Tank, Get Down and DC, sitting on the porch. It was their every morning routine, meeting on the front porch with the rise of the sun, to have a drink amongst the crew.

"Aey Spider, man you here about that cat that got popped last night over on Lucille," DC asked him.

"Who?"

"Shit, Hawk 'nem laid that nigga Slick down sideways, you hear me," DC said, hitting the half pint of grape MD 20/20 on the bottom with his palm before popping the top.

"These nigga's gon' learn to quit fuckin' with mutherfucka's shit. Slick broke into Hawk's 'nem house the night before last and stole all kinds of shit. Even the muthafuckin' copper out the basement. Hawk 'nem followed his ass from F&G's last night and stretched his ass out. Heard they shot all the nigga's fingers off before they shot him in the head," Get Down said, taking a swallow of the purple wine.

"Damn, these nigga's ain't playin'. They lettin' them bells ring around this bitch like it ain't shit," Spider said, reaching down the front of his shorts to retrieve his weed from underneath his balls.

"Hol' on, I gotta go handle somethin'."

Spider walked across Mimika Avenue to the brown and white brick home where Man was sitting on the porch with his uncle.

"What's good, Man? What's good, Unc?" Spider said as he climbed the steps and gave them love.

"Sppiiddeerr," Man sang as he reached in his pocket for a twenty dollar bill. Spider watched as Man peeled the twenty from a thick wad of cash.

"Damn nigga, the boy business keepin' you fat ain't it?"

"Uhh, basically," Man said, smiling.

They exchanged goods and Spider took a seat on the edge of the porch rail. As Spider sat chit-chatting with his neighbors and customers, gun shots rang out.

Pop, pop, pop, pop.

They all hit the porch ground. Bullets in the hood know no faces and have no names written on them. The sounds of the screeching tires along with the silence in the air let them know the drama was over...or so they thought.

"Damn, did ya'll hear them shots," the voice asked as they all stood to their feet, dusting off their clothes. They turned to greet their neighbor, Punkin, as she stood in the doorway of her grey and black home.

Punkin was the perfect neighbor, if you lived in the hood cause she was simply just "*ghetto by nature.*" She was the kind of neighbor that you could sit around and chill with, smoke a couple of blunts, get your drink on and get all the latest gossip, all at the same time.

She was always in the mist of things. Punkin was so nosey, you didn't need to watch the news or pick up the *Evening Whirl* to find out information on what went down in the hood. All you had to do was show up, ready to smoke and get an entire ear full.

"DAMN," Spider said, brushing the porch dirt off his white-tee.

"Who the fuck poppin' that thang this damn early in the mornin'?"

"Aey ya'll, it's a nigga lyin' on the lot over there next to Lil Curtis 'nem house," Punkin said, pointing to the corner of Mimika and Shulte.

They all started walking down to the sidewalk as a crowd began to gather at the corner. Get Down, Tank and DC came running across the block to make sure their home boy was alright.

"Shit nigga, we thought you was toast!" DC said, hitting Spider on the back.

"Fuck that! The only thing toast round this muthafucka is my drank! A nigga dropped it when them rounds went off."

Spider reached for the MD in DC's hand, turned it up and took it straight to the head. As he turned back towards the porch, out the corner of his eye, he saw her.

Standing on Punkin's steps with her hair pulled up in a ponytail, dressed in a soft pink capri's and a pink floral cami, was Punkin's youngest sister, Mystic.

Spider had seen her before when he'd brought medicine over to Punkin and her crew but for the most part, they had never said much to each other past "hi and bye."

Mystic was gorgeous to him. Five-five, 160 pounds of thickness, beautiful skin, pretty hands and gorgeous feet. Spider loved a woman with pretty feet. He couldn't stand a woman to wear sandals in the summer time with jacked up feet, lookin' like she'd been busting concrete with her heels.

Mystic waved to him as she came down the steps.

"Hey mommy," Spider said.

"Hey Spider, what happened," she asked, approaching him.

"Some nigga got popped."

"In broad daylight," she asked, folding her arms.

Mystic found the hood life so exciting. She was used to the living the life of a sheltered military wife and mother. Used to the type of neighborhoods where people left their front doors wide open all night and no one would step foot inside their homes. Although the best environment for raising a family, she hated the staleness of the military life and Mystic longed for a life filled with excitement and adventure.

She wanted a "soldier..," not Uncle Sam's illegitimate sons but a real soldier… a hood nigga, a thug-a-boo (a thug-a-boo is a nigga whose gutta on the outside but soft on the inside when it come to his woman). Mystic wanted someone to protect her and make her feel safe. Someone she could share her deepest secrets with and know that he'd make it his business to make it better. Someone who bore the word "Strength" across their chest like a finely pinned tattoo.

Mystic saw all the things she wanted in Spider, yet she was also afraid of him. Afraid of some of the bullshit she had heard about him, afraid of the life style everyone said he led. She was afraid mostly because she was already on federal probation and couldn't risk going back to prison for anyone or any reason, no matter how fine he was.

Mystic longed to get her daughter back, the one taken from her when she was arrested eight years ago. Her daughter was only two years old when Mystic last laid eyes on her and she missed her terribly. Mystic had allowed he ex-husband to talk her into going a check cashing scam that went bogus and ended up yielding her six years away from those she loved the most. Getting her daughter back would take Mystic jumping through many hoops and walking a line so straight, stumbling to the left or the right even slightly, could cost her, he daughter forever.

She couldn't risk getting into trouble again for anyone. She had to stay clean, even if that meant fighting the desire for the streets and her dream of both loving and being loved by a bad boy.

"Well mommy, that's how it goes down in the hood. Gangsta shit don't respect no time of day," Spider said, touching her arm.

Mystic felt a tingle go down her spine. She sank down into his touch.

"Umm, should I go and call for help?"

"Naw, I'm sure somebody already did. I'll tell you what you should do, you should let me take you to dinner cause, I think I like you."

Mystic smiled.

She looked Spider in his eyes and wondered if he could see her soul crying out to him.

"I think I like you too but I can't let you take me to dinner," Mystic said, thinking to herself, *damn this nigga is so fucking fine.*

"Why not?"

"Cause," she paused.

"You're a bad boy Spider, I can't mess with you. I say probation and your lifestyle is like playin' Russian roulette with my freedom and I ain't tryin' to see them Feds again," she said, walking away.

Spider grabbed her by the arm.

"Mommy. I would never have you around anything that I do. I would never jeopardize you in any way, trust that. You think I wanna see you caged in? Now, take my number and call me."

Mystic wanted to walk away again but her thirst to know what it felt like to be loved by a thug overwhelmed her. She took out her cell phone and recorded his number inside.

"Gon' inside, you don't need to be around this shit and nigga's round here believe in round trip tickets," he told her.

"Round trip?" Mystic looked at him confused.

"Meanin', they might round the corner and slide through again. Especially if they wanna make sure that nigga dead."

She turned to walk away and smiled to herself. Mystic liked the way he had just commanded her to go indoors; she liked the forcefulness in his voice. She turned back to him and waved as she went inside.

"Aey Spider, nigga that's Kay Kay stretched out on that lot," Get Down said, out of breath from running across the street.

"What? My nigga, Kay Kay?"

"Yep. Looks bad too man," he told Spider.

Spider sprinted across the street as Mystic watched him through the window. When he reached his friend, Spider kneeled down and lifted him upon his lap.

"My cat, what's good?"

Kay Kay gave no response. He gripped Spider's left arm and opened his mouth to speak but the only thing escaping from his lips was the gush of blood. Kay Kay squeezed Spider's arm tighter and tighter. He was gasping for air as the blood flowed from his body. He had been shot in the stomach, the left leg and his right shoulder.

He was dying right there in Spider's arms.

"Who did this man? Who did this to you? Answer me... Kay, answer me."

Kay Kay's signs of life were slipping, fast. Spider felt a tear fall from his eyes as he watched his childhood friend's life slip away. Kay Kay was dead and Spider was in rage. He wiped the blood from his hand and closed his friend's eyes. He vowed to his friend that he would find out who was responsible and make them pay. No matter when, no matter where he found them, he would make them pay...on that you could bet.

Other Novels

By

Allysha Hamber

The NorthSide Clit
Keep It On The Down Low
What's Done In The Dark

..Coming Soon..

Mimika Avenue
The NorthSide Clit 2
Unlovable Bitch 2

You can reach the Author at:
Email: lele4you@hotmail.com
www.myspace.com/allyshahamber

Made in the USA